ISBN-13: 9798346098430

Cover design by Marley Free
Printed in the United States of America

Seven Secrets for Capturing the Heart of Mr. Right

by Marley Free

Prologue

C assidy was pan-frying a batch of conveniently frozen potstickers when she noticed Bootles digging under the Blushing Akito roses again. "Amanda!" she yelled, "Can you please go get Bootles? He's after the roses again!" Since having moved in nine days ago, Bootles had been obsessed with those particular rose bushes. Who could blame him? They provided a gorgeous pink pop to their back yard where Cassidy fantasized about hosting outdoor birthday parties for Amanda, or for herself, or hopefully one day a child of their own. One of the most appealing aspects of this property was its backyard with its beautiful landscaping and potential for outdoor entertaining. Because of this, Cassidy had prodded Amanda, "Please, let's put in the extra ten thousand over asking. It's only a few dollars a month when you spread it over thirty years." Cassidy had never been a real gardener, but she vowed to become one now that she had the space for it.

The thumping sound of Amanda's socked feet trotting down the stairs jerked Cassidy out of her party-hosting daydream and back into reality. She grasped the cardboard box from the frozen potstickers laying on the kitchen counter and quickly crumpled it, shoving it into the bottom of the trashcan. Amanda probably knew they were frozen, but Cassidy liked it when Amanda assumed that Cassidy's dinners were homemade. Cassidy kept the convenience-food evidence out of sight in order to support this illusion in which Amanda may or may not have been participating.

"I got 'em" Amanda said, slipping on her heavy workboots and starting to trudge outside. "Bootles, watchu got?" Amanda yelled to the snorting pug, whose bright white fur was now caked with mud and mulch. Bootles' cartoonishly shining black eyes met Amanda's as he bounded toward her with hope of a big hug, extra petting, and admiration for the gift he grasped in his teeth, his floppy lips cascading over a chunk of something brown and green. Amanda wrestled the chunk out of Bootles' slobbery mouth, but didn't recognize its origin.

Amanda examined the sticky mass until she felt an uncomfortable realization coming over her. She tossed the foreign object and picked up Bootles, who was panting and struggling to get back to his rosebed discovery mission.

"Hon, is everything okay?" Cassidy asked, coming toward Amanda and Bootles.

"I think we need to call somebody" Amanda said, gruffly. The three of them peered at the object on the ground, which was identified later that evening as a broken-off human sternum, its costal cartilage half-putrified and still clinging to the bone.

Chapter One

Break Up With Him if He Doesn't Flaunt You

March 2013

As Laurie and Matthew walked up to Matthew's condo, Laurie's flowing floral blouse swayed with the pendulous swing of her hips. She put one foot in front of the other, letting her wedge slip ons lead the way for each other, as if creating a perforated line, just the way that she had read once that runway models walked. She listened for the rhythm of her shoes more than she was listening to Matthew talk about their family dog and how cute she had been as a puppy. Before Laurie had been to Matthew's condo, Laurie had assumed this dog was solely Matthew's dog and not in fact his parents' dog because he always referred to the pup as "his dog."Laurie only halfway acknowledged Matthew's indication of his puppy-tooth shaped scars on his arm. Laurie wasn't thinking about the dog, or Matthew, or dinner at all. Laurie was thinking about Matthew's mother, whom Laurie would be meeting tonight. This was the only reason she chose a floral shirt and omitted her usual thick line of black eyeliner below her lower lashes. Based on the way Matthew talked about his mother, she knew that this meeting had to go well. Matthew and Laurie had been dating for one year and Laurie had given Matthew an ultimatum two weeks ago. "It's weird," she told him, "that your family is so important to you, but you haven't introduced me to them. Do they even know that I exist? Do they know they're meeting me tonight?"

"Yeah, haha, well, no, I guess I haven't really said anything. It's just that, well, they're really protective of me and I care about you and I don't want them to scare you away."

Laurie had often wondered if Matthew was embarrassed by the additional weight she carried compared to other women on dating apps. It didn't matter now though, because Laurie would be meeting Matthew's parents at dinner tonight. They ascended the three flights of stairs and made their way to Matthew's door.

"Oh, wow. That's a nice Easter wreath." Laurie told Matthew, pushing aside her slight and inexplicable discomfort that a thirty year old bachelor would purchase an Easter wreath.

"Thanks. My mom got it for me. She always does stuff like that. So, what do you want to get for dinner?" he asked as he unlocked the deadbolt.

"Anything. What do your folks like?" She paused. "Honestly, I thought maybe you had cooked or ordered something ahead; I would have brought something and helped set up but you were pretty insistent that I not worry about it. What time are they coming? Should we go back downstairs and get some wine from across the street?" Matthew walked through the door and Laurie's concern grew as she followed him into the living room. She wondered how much time they had to get a full dinner together.

Matthew sighed. "They can't make it tonight, so it's just us."

"What?" Laurie asked, shaking her head and leaning forward slightly. "When did they cancel? Or.. Wait.. Did you *actually* invite them to come?"

"Well, I did, but, I didn't actually tell them about you, so no, I didn't actually end up inviting them, I guess."

Matthew expected Laurie to respond immediately so that he wouldn't have to find his next words. She stayed silent and waited for him to continue, "I'm sorry. I know I said I would. I just chickened out I guess."

Part of Laurie had thought this would happen, but she was really hoping that part of her would be wrong.

"So, wanna get Thai? I could go for some Pad See Ew tonight. And spring rolls."

Laurie exhaled. "Sure. That sounds good. I think I'm gonna get red curry tonight" she said neutrally.

"You're not mad, are you?" Matthew asked her. Laurie hated it when Matthew asked her about her feelings as if making an accusation.

"Well, yeah, I feel a little mad. We agreed that you were going to introduce me to your parents tonight and you're acting like it's no big deal that you disregarded our agreement."

"I see." said Matthew.

Chiang Mai Thai delivered some mediocre noodles, which Laurie and Matthew ate throughout mild and shallow conversation.

"Oh! I've got dessert!" Matthew exclaimed, almost falling out of his chair.

"Oh, nice-"

"My mom made cookies. They're great. She makes the best cookies." Matthew retrieved and opened a red plastic container revealing about two dozen shortbread circles with spoon-pressed indentations in their centers, which were filled with an orange, glossy goop. "They're peach. They're so good. Have one! I'll be right back." Matthew made a beeline for the powder room.

He often sought a toilet immediately after eating.

Laurie heard the dinging sounds of Matthew's phone as he began a game of Bejeweled underscored by the low roar of the bathroom fan. When this happened, Matthew was usually absent for ten to twenty-five minutes. Laurie looked at the container of cookies and silent rage made her fingertips itch. She shoved a cookie in her mouth. The shortbread didn't have the crumbly quality of a cookie that had been made with butter; the cookie squished under her teeth, clearly having been crafted from margarine or seed oil. The peach center was pleasant, almost offering a richness of a deep caramel. Laurie took the container of cookies and set them to the right of the oversized kitchen basin. Laurie loved the features of the kitchen at Matthew's condo, but there was usually an unpleasant stickiness on various surfaces and smeary residue on the handles of the refrigerator and microwave. She often found herself collecting chip crumbs and wiping counters and appliances without realizing it. Lately she had been making an effort to stop herself whenever she noticed that she was improving the living space. Laurie opened the cabinet under the kitchen sink. There she saw the box of ant baits that she had purchased three months ago and stuck in the back behind the bottles of cleaning products which Matthew never touched. She squatted and reached to the back of the cabinet, grasping the box and pulling it out. Laurie had purchased the ant baits after noticing a trail of ants coming in from the kitchen window and parading around the toaster. She had neither set them up though, nor suggested to Matthew that he use them, mostly because she felt it would be overstepping the one-year girlfriend/boyfriend boundaries that don't deteriorate until two or three years of being together. Laurie also knew that Matthew adored animals, including the insects in his home. This was actually one of the qualities she loved about him. Whenever they would go on walks he would laugh with delight at the sighting of common critters, especially squirrels and chipmunks. After purchasing the ant baits and thinking more deeply about them, Laurie thought Matthew might be offended by them, perceiving their existence as cruel. They were designed to lure the ants into a chamber of sweet and delicious poison, which they would sample, collect, and haul back to their colonies, feeding and thus killing the whole community, from the tiniest infant ant to the mighty ant queen.

Laurie worked quickly, retrieving kitchen shears from the second lowest drawer next to the refrigerator. Matthew seemed unaware of the drawers in the kitchen, excluding the top ones, as the lower ones were filled with unused kitchen linens and new-in-plastic kitchen gadgets that he didn't know he owned. She opened the box of ant baits and tore open the plastic wrapping of all eight of them. One by one, she carefully cut through the exterior vertical sides of the plastic ant hallways and shimmied the tops off of the ant baits. She imagined ants looking up as if their sky dome were opening for the first time. She didn't know if that's how the ants would react to seeing her, but she imagined them cowering before her, wondering how best they could appease her to save their lives. With a spoon, Laurie scooped the tan-colored gel out of each ant bait and combined the gel with the peachy center of the top eight cookies in the plastic container. They looked almost identical to the original cookies, just a little more full. Laurie gathered the trash from the ant baits and folded it all together carefully into a compact mass, which she slid into the flattened cardboard box that had housed the traps until that evening. She stuck the trash at the bottom of her bag.

Laurie waited. She pulled out her phone and went through her usual mindless rotation of checking her email, her Instagram, her work email, and back again to her personal email. She then redownloaded the LoveHappens app. She remembered deleting LoveHappens after she had spoken with Matthew and they concluded that they were, in fact, an official relationship and were not just casually dating. She remembered the conversation very well. They were eating frozen yogurt in the food court of the mall after seeing the movie *American Sniper*.

"So, hey, I've been thinking lately that I am enjoying hanging out with you, but I'm really wondering about the direction this is going in." said Laurie.

"I was just thinking the same thing!"

"Wow! I'm relieved. I wasn't sure we were on the same page."

"So... Are we... An official item?" Laurie asked, hoping that Matthew would cut in with something reassuring. Matthew stared blankly at Laurie. It seemed they were not on the same page. Matthew shoveled the last half-cup of rainbow gummy bear soft serve into his mouth.

"Give me a couple days to think about it," said Matthew, his mouth still full of the once colorful yogurt, which had now melded into a grey bolus full of gummy chunks. "I'll let you know then."

The rustle of denim rising from the bathroom floor began the familiar song-like sequence of Matthew's emergence from the bathroom. The last notes of the doorknob turning and the door hinges squawking cued Matthew's reappearance, giving Laurie's brain enough time to transition out of flashback mode and back into the present.

"Did you have a cookie?" Matthew asked Laurie excitedly.

"I had two. Thank you." Laurie told Matthew, smiling, her phone-free hand becoming clammy under the table. She repeatedly wiped the sweat onto her pants. Matthew picked up a cookie in each hand. He devoured one and then put the second one in his mouth as soon as he had swallowed the first.

"Theth aw tho gooh." Matthew said, his mouth so full that

the cookies did all of the articulating for him. Laurie noted the receipt from the Thai food; she calmly picked it up and folded it four times into a tiny rectangle, which she filed at the bottom of her jeans pocket. Matthew ate all eight of the adjusted cookies and two of the original recipe ones. Upon finishing the second non-poisoned cookie, Matthew looked at the remaining cookies.

"Oh no." Laurie thought. "He's wondering why they taste different. There's a huge difference in color and sheen. Why in the world would I think he might not notice?" Laurie's lower back began to sweat and her floral blouse clung to her midsection, the droplets adhering the fabric to her sweaty skin.

"Wanna watch a movie or something?" Matthew asked.

"Sure!" Laurie said, tilting her head slightly toward her left shoulder and smiling. They left the saucy takeout containers strewn on the table where they had eaten and relocated to the once-white sofa, which had acquired more and more soda and beer stains in its young life than the owner of a white sofa should ever allow. Matthew scrolled through the movies available for streaming.

"Wanna watch Final Destination?" Matthew had old-horror-film desire in his eyes.

"Yes!" She said, even though she did not care to see the film.

After the opening credits, Matthew rubbed his stomach. He shifted back and forth and then rubbed it again. He sat for a second and then pressed his palms into his obliques, as if trying to straighten out wrinkles from his shirt. A few seconds went by and then he did it again. He scooted back on the sofa, like he was trying to force his buttcheeks into the crease where the back cushions met the seat cushions. He stayed there for four seconds and then thrusted his hips forward, bringing himself up to a standing position. "I don't feel good" he said. "Do you feel okay after that Thai food?"

"I'm feeling fine." Laurie said, picking up the remote and pausing the movie, offering her best concerned facial expression. "Are you not feeling so well?"

"I feel kind of sick." Matthew grunted, beginning to pace back and forth in front of the couch between Laurie and the television. He swept off a few beads of sweat from his forehead using his right forearm. Mid-step, Matthew stopped pacing. He had one foot pointed behind him and it looked like he was trying to screw his big toe into the floor. His shoulders tensed back and his arms went forward. He spread his fingers like he was trying to hold onto the air.

"Maybe you should sit down." Laurie told him. She got up and led him back to the couch. He sat down and then slumped over onto his side. Matthew tried various positions on the couch, seeking a comfortable arrangement, but his constant motion reminded Laurie of one of those colorful flailing tube air dancers commonly used to grab the attention of passersby at car dealerships and other gimmicky businesses. When Matthew spiraled toward the back of the couch, his head planting itself in the corner, Laurie subtly grabbed Matthew's cell phone from the coffee table and zipped into the kitchen. She committed to the first place that registered in her brain as somewhere Matthew wouldn't look for his phone: the toaster. She was back by his side before he noticed she had stepped away.

Matthew squirmed and writhed. Face-up, he found a second of peace and let his back dip into the couch cushions, but the pain returned immediately and he pushed his hips upward into a bridge. "I have to get to the bathroom" he said, clenching all of his muscles.

Laurie put her arm under his and wrapped it around his back, helping to support him. He moved as if the Nile were trying to escape his bowels. They made their way to the bathroom and Matthew shut the door behind him. Chunky liquid spewed from Matthew in every way it could forge. After twenty minutes, Laurie knocked on the door.

"How are you doing in there?" she asked.

"Not so good" he said.

"Do you need anything?" she asked.

"I think I should drink some water."

"Do you think you can keep a little water down?"

"I don't know, but I'm going to dehydrate if I don't try."

"Do you want something with some electrolytes? I can run down to the convenience store and get you a Gatorade."

"Yes. Please." He chirped. Laurie hurried down the condominium building stairs and headed to the convenience store on the corner. When she approached the refrigerated sports beverages, she reached past her favorite flavor: lemon-lime, and Matthew's favorite flavor: orange, to select the bluest drink she could see: Arctic Breeze. She bought two of them and instead of returning to Matthew's smelly loo, she speed-walked to her car. From Laurie's pocket, she opened the trunk with her car key remote. When she reached the car, she stuck the Gatorades inside the trunk and looked around to see if anybody was watching. Laurie opened one of the bottles and poured half of it on the pavement below her car. She brought the half full bottle back up to the trunk and worked under her flannel blanket that she kept in there in case her car ever broke down and it was cold outside. Laurie felt for and located the large jug of antifreeze that she also kept in there. She filled the bottle to the brim and rescrewed the cap. Laurie shoved the regular sports drink and the tainted one in her bag, shut the trunk of her car, and headed back up to sick Matthew.

"Do you want to see if you can keep some sports drink

down?" Laurie asked Matthew.

"Yeah." He opened the bathroom door just wide enough for his pale and shaky hand to reach through and flop around the door jamb, feeling around for the bottle like a trout on a fishing boat looking for an exit from a cooler of shallow water. He grasped the bottle, pulled it inside the bathroom with him, and snapped the door shut. Laurie heard Matthew sip the antifreeze cocktail. Sip. Another sip. A gulp. Laurie had read on the child safety warning label that antifreeze tastes sweet, but she wasn't sure how close it was in taste to blue Gatorade. Matthew didn't seem to notice anything out of the ordinary, but his palate wasn't the most astute to begin with, and the ant poison's effect on Matthew's stomach and intestines didn't leave him much mental room for mindfully tasting the beverage. Who was to say what "Arctic Breeze" tasted like anyway? Laurie imagined that an "Arctic Breeze" flavored beverage would taste like cold fish and greasy penguin feathers. The actual flavor tasted like something made in a lab with unknown inspiration. Matthew's "Arctic Breeze" must have tasted like antifreeze, which would soon begin to crystallize within his organs and shut down his kidneys. The beverage had already begun to affect Matthew's lungs and central nervous system. Laurie grimaced as she heard him take little gasps of air and repeatedly flop against the tile floor of the bathroom after each failed attempt of pulling himself up using the toilet bowl.

Laurie decided to go for a walk to get some fresh air. When she returned, it would be time for the real work to begin.

Laurie put Matthew's home key in the lock and slowly turned the deadbolt. She opened the door about a foot wide and listened carefully. Nothing. Entering and silently closing the door behind her, she locked the deadbolt and listened again. Still nothing. Laurie slowly walked toward the living room and sat on the couch. She waited for two minutes, being careful not to breathe audibly. She still didn't hear any shuffling or moaning or scratching or crying, which was a relief. Laurie stood up and slowly crept toward the door of the powder room. The light was still on and the fan was still running diligently. Laurie had better give him just a little more time. She returned to the couch and put on an episode of *Modern Family*. This was a show that she was able to enjoy without giving it her full attention. She referred to this type of programming as "laundry TV," because she could happy walk around her home completing mindless chores and tasks, like laundry, while relishing the witty banter and the humor coming from the show's ridiculous situations, like when the middle-aged suburban characters Phil and Claire adopted fabricated personas that made them feel adventurous enough to have sex in a hotel and then Claire got the belt of her trench coat stuck in the escalator and she couldn't remove the coat because she was naked underneath it. That was funny.

After watching an episode by herself, Laurie turned off the television and listened carefully. She still heard the normal sounds of the apartment and the dull roaring of the bathroom fan. She sat for a few more minutes until her own breathing seemed loud to her. Laurie stood up and took small steps toward the door of the bathroom, listening between each step for sounds of movement. When she reached the bathroom door, she gently pressed an ear to it and closed her eyes. She couldn't make out any breathing or twitching. She knocked. There was no response. She opened the door a crack and saw Matthew's pale cheeks completely at rest, no longer holding any natural tension. There was a small puddle of pale pink-tinged drool that had leaked onto the tile floor from Matthew's open mouth.

"Hey" Laurie whispered. Matthew didn't move. His eyes were open. "Hey" she said at a low volume. Still no response. He was gone.

It took a while for Laurie to remove Matthew from the bathroom but when they arrived back in the living room, she placed Matthew on his left side with his face toward the television so that he could enjoy the next episode of Modern Family that she would put on for background noise. She felt a little bad that he had missed the last episode while he was in the bathroom. She picked up Matthew's right leg and rotated it, envisioning the femoral head rolling within his pelvis. It would be difficult to dislocate his hips, but it was the only way to begin. Ball and socket joints were tricky. Pop! When she pulled hard at just right right angle, she felt the bones release their embrace. Laurie found that the best way to do this was to lie on the floor with her head facing Matthew's shins and her feet consequently tip-toeing on his face. She brought her right leg up to Matthew's crotch and leveraged her force, grasping his leg against her chest and pulling it while pushing against the center of his pelvis. The other leg was easier once she had been through the technique once successfully. "Sorry, Matt," she apologized. "You can't see the TV anymore but I need you in this position. It's okay. Don't fall apart on me." Laurie continued dislocating joints and hearing eerily satisfying pops, like she was cracking her own knuckles and releasing the pressure between bones. Except for the pops signifying progress, she wasn't enjoying the process. It felt gross and risky. It was too late to turn back though; she had to clean up her mess. She couldn't unkill Matthew and leave him happily eating Thai noodles like he was only eight hours ago. She wished she had just broken up with him and left to watch TV at her townhouse. She could have been asleep right now instead of formulating her "body disposal plan," a phrase which fit the circumstances in two ways. Laurie could have chuckled.

The cutting was the worst part. Laurie lifted Matthew to the oversized kitchen basin, first with many unsuccessful tries, the most gruesome one being when his nostril caught on the handle of the lower cabinet. She would have to remember to clean that up, just in case anybody would examine the kitchen hardware. She made the biggest cuts first. With Matthew's largest butcher knife from his collection, still as pristine as its day of purchase, Laurie hacked away at the shallow ditches she had formed in Matthew's upper legs from dislocating his hip joints. The blood, thin at first, with streams of thicker, darker blood following gurgled down the drain.

Laurie had only seen garbage disposals like the one Matthew had in commercial kitchens and luxurious mansions, but for some reason, Matthew's condo featured an InSinkErator 2 HP disposal, an almost $3000 item. She had pondered the placement of this garbage disposal, but she and Matthew had never conversed about it. She wondered if it was another kitchen gem that he glossed over daily without utilizing or appreciating. Probably. There were professional chefs in the world yearning for this garbage disposal, yet Matthew would never use it, that is, until now.

Laurie decided to warm up the disposal a little before forcing it into the heavy lifting it was about to do. She turned on the only switch she saw, which turned out to be a deliberately placed post-modern lighting fixture that she hadn't actually noticed until now. "Oh yeah," she thought. "The disposal switch is under the sink." Laurie was starting to get tired. "The femurs will be the worst," she thought, "So it would be best to start with something a little smaller just in case the disposal breaks and I have to go to Plan B." She didn't have a Plan B yet. Laurie finished most of the cutting, finding that Matthew's large serrated knife, also from his semi-professional butcher block, would practically glide back and forth through the tougher muscle and sinews if she sliced in at about a 30 degree angle. Laurie hoped Matthew's neighbors wouldn't complain about the ninety minutes of on-and-off garbage disposal sounds, or worse, come knocking on the door to check on the noises.

All of the bones, except one, were eventually able to make their way down the dark tunnel at the bottom of the sink, reminding Laurie of mountain climbers repelling down the rocks of a vertical descent, mostly in the way that some of the longer bones like the radius and ulna clanked against the sides of the disposal entrance. The rib cage had given her some trouble but she was able to chip away at it piece by piece.

The skull was another story. Laurie looked around Matthew's condo for something heavy to smash his skull with. There weren't any marble bookends or large planters to be found. She searched the kitchen and settled on the knife block itself. She unloaded all of the knives that weren't already out getting some exercise and she wrapped Matthew's head in the plastic tote bag that their Thai food had arrived in earlier. Laurie raised the empty knife block up high over her head and then brought it down, colliding with Matthew's skull. Nothing. Again. She was worried that she might break a kitchen tile in the process. In her third attempt, Laurie heard a crack and the process got easier from there. The experience reminded her of breaking open a coconut from the grocery store, which she remembered having taken a very long time for the actual amount of edible coconut inside. Just as Laurie stuck to canned coconut from that experience on, Laurie promised she would never do this again. "Impulsive. Sloppy. Stupid" she thought as she bleached all of the kitchen surfaces, washed the materials she used for Matthew's disposal, and packed up the surprisingly little amount of trash to toss in an out-of-the-way dumpster. "I deserve to get caught."

Laurie needed a nap, a bottle of wine, and a reboot for her nervous system. Today was going to be one of those just-get-through-it-hang-in-there-until-it's-time-to-go-home-and-that-will be-your-only-accomplishment-and-that's-good-enough kind of days. It was expected that Laurie show her face in the office at least three times a week, even if it was just to pick up materials or attend the weekly team meeting, but Laurie had only been in once this week. She had to go in today and make sure that she could be spotted visibly working: making phone calls, writing emails, ordering glossy mailers, drinking coffee, or making lists. Pretending to do many of these things was just as good as actually doing them when it came to her image at work.

Laurie walked into the office and breathed a sigh of relief. Nobody else was there yet. She let her posture fall into a slump and she shuffled across the short looped carpet toward the kitchenette. She started a make a pot of coffee and look around. She had noticed immediately that there was a bakery box from the doughnut shop around the corner. She looked at them through the translucent plastic window of the box top to see that they were just as glossy as the enormous pile of future junk mail she was supposed to mail today but had never actually ordered like she had meant to do at the beginning of the week. Whoops. Laurie's head was pounding from the lack of a good night's sleep. It was almost like she was watching herself go through the motions in a very boring movie instead of living and acting as herself. She wondered if the doughnuts were from yesterday or from the day before that. She lifted the box top with her right index finger and took a peek. It wasn't worth it; these doughnuts might have been three days old. The good ones obviously disappeared first; the Boston cream, chocolate cake flavored, and classic glazed were all long gone only leaving a raspberry jelly filled, a blueberry, and and a festive St. Patrick's Day one with green sprinkles. Laurie pulled her finger back and let the top of the box fall closed. While the coffee brewed, she went back to the desk where she most often worked and opened the bottom right filing drawer, one of the few places she had claimed as her own. Each professional in the office had a few spots for storing their things, which everybody knew and respected, even though technically all of the workspaces were communal and anybody was allowed to work anywhere. She retrieved her notebook, which she usually took him with her, but had forgotten last time. When Laurie had trouble getting momentum going at work, it usually helped her to make a to-do list. She wasn't sure whether or not it actually made her accomplish more tasks, but she definitely felt more organized and less like she was flailing around trying to take care of duties as she thought of them, like playing a game off office-drone whack-a-mole. Laurie at least liked how she felt when she could look at the crossed-out items and remember that she had made some accomplishments, however small they were. In times when she felt stressed and wondered if she could get everything done that she needed to, she looked back at lists from the past and smiled with satisfaction at the crossed out items and the evidence that everything had been resolved, even though she had been feeling the same type of stress at those times. Laurie took her notebook and pen from the desk and she headed back toward the kitchenette where she left her Allington Liberty Group canvas tote bag, which only contained her purse that she had shoved in there this morning. She checked her phone and rolled her shoulders back in comfort that there weren't any additional voicemails or emails to add to her list yet. She opened her notebook to a fresh, clean page and wrote the date at the top right-hand corner, just like children are trained to do in school. A small form of stalling happened next, when she titled the list "To Do," as if she could otherwise confuse the list at some point with her grocery list and end up calling Mr. Plumcourt to follow up about his recent home inspection instead of buying bananas.

Laurie listed the phone calls she needed to make today. She listed the emails she needed to compose. She listed the different types of mailers she needed to order. She listed the same mailers she hadn't designed yet and wrote "Pull photos and fill in design templates" for each one. She looked up at the fluorescent light in the kitchenette and arched her back, cracking three of her upper vertebrae. She felt a little better after emptying the scurrying tasks from her brain and containing them in the notebook, like capturing rats whose cages had been left open in a laboratory and putting them back in their places, transforming the space from chaos into a land of productivity and discovery. Laurie looked back at the doughnuts. She was hungry. She stood still for a moment and then her hand went into the box. She picked up the hardened blueberry doughnut and dropped it back in its place to hear the type of thud that it made. These doughnuts were definitely older than yesterday. The coffee had finally finished brewing and she retrieved her go-to teal mug from the upper cabinet to pour herself some caffeination. She looked in the fridge. Damn. There wasn't any cream. Laurie had brought in whipping cream last week, mainly for her own use, but she was always willing to share. Other office compadres usually brought in sugary flavored vegetable-oil-based creamers or sometimes skim milk, and she hated both of those in her coffee. Laurie sighed and took a sip of her black coffee. Hot. Gross. She exhaled, trying to cool down her mouth. Laurie wanted the energizing benefit of the coffee, but she didn't feel like drinking the bitter, thin liquid. She grabbed the crusty blueberry donut and dunked it into the sad coffee. She took a big bite of the coffee-soaked softened pastry and chewed. She dunked the doughnut again, but this time took a bite of the coffee-less side, avoiding the bitter, undressed liquid. Laurie had finished the doughnut before taking another sip of the coffee, which now registered as gross to her. Laurie thought about how long it had probably been since the coffee machine had been cleaned, if ever. Unfiltered tap water trickling through a second hand Mr. Coffee and dripping onto generic pre-ground discount beans just wasn't cutting it today. Laurie felt hungover and the substandard coffee was just too acidic. Laurie ate the other two doughnuts to try and feel better. It didn't work. She folded the dirty doughnut box four times and tucked it in the trash can, moving two napkins to cover up its exposed edge. The bright orange corner of the bakery box still peeked through a little bit, like a hidden Easter egg of shame peaking out from under a bush.

The rest of the day was about as pleasurable as Laurie's acidic and bitter coffee. It was overcast, and the HVAC system seemed louder than usual. Laurie trudged through, thinking that eventually she'd see a coworker, but nobody showed up. At 4:00 pm, Laurie shoved her notebook in her canvas tote and headed out. Instead of going straight to her car, however, she stopped at the liquor store and bought one bottle of wine and one bottle of vodka.

Laurie made herself a grilled cheese while she drank large gulps of sauvignon blanc out of her biggest, most bulbus piece of stemware. She ate half of the sandwich and carefully arranged the rest in a glass storage container, which she placed squarely in her refrigerator. She poured herself another glass of wine, the second third of the bottle. She took a deep breath. Another gulp. Another ice cube. Laurie only added ice cubes to her white wine when nobody was around to watch. She opened the refrigerator again and retrieved the square glass storage container with the blue silicone top. She pried the top off of the container and placed it on the middle shelf of the fridge. Laurie held the refrigerator door open with her right elbow while she stared at the back of the refrigerator wall and finished the rest of the no longer crispy sandwich, which had reached room temperature.

Staring at the empty glass container and the lid, which she had just placed in the sink, Laurie thought about taking a bath. While she usually enjoyed a warm bath once she was in it, the pleasure was fleeting. She didn't enjoy looking down at her naked body soaking in the water. She imagined her outer layer of dead skin cells sloughing off and greying the water slightly, creating something like a live human broth. Laurie didn't like being a soup. She polished off the bottle of wine and trodded up the stairs. As soon as she reached the last step, she unbuttoned the button of her jeans and let the zipper unclench more and more of its staggered teeth as she walked into her bedroom, swaying her hips along the way. The pants reached the ground and she kicked them toward her hamper in the corner of the room. Laurie's very inviting bed hugged her as she dove in. Her arms embraced one of her four pillows and she dragged it down next to her. Finally, peace. Laurie rested her eyelids for two minutes. The muscles in her face relaxed, so if a stranger had been watching, the stranger would have thought Laurie looked tired and mean, rather than restful. Laurie put a lot of her daily energy into looking cheerful and upbeat, always ready to answer questions and greet her next prospective client. Laurie turned onto her back. Her hands found her hip bones and she ran her fingers along the front sides of her pelvis from under a soft fold of skin. Her thumbs led her hands to the small of her back and she rolled her shoulders into the mattress, stretching and lengthening her spine. Laurie's hips moved up and down, as if they were briskly using a stair-stepper at the gym. Then she exhaled and stayed still. Her fingertips gingerly crawled under the elastic waistband of her underwear and massaged the fleshy trenches where her inner thighs ramped up to her outer labia. She spread herself open with her left hand and let her right index finger lead the way to her clitoris. A few laps around with her finger and she was dipping down into her vulva to gather her natural lubrication, which heightened her clitoris, like an intrigued mountain. She pressed a little harder and fell into a rhythmic, circular strum. She didn't want to reach her destination too quickly, so she slowed down, as only about ninety seconds had passed since her fingers had started their swim in their favorite lake. Laurie stalled the journey before her climax by alternating between gently tapping the summit of her clitoris and giving the star of the show a little break by sliding her finger into her vagina and slowly stirring, as if it were a rubber spatula gathering the last ribbons of brownie batter clinging to the sides of a mixing bowl. Her left hand traveled up to massage her large, soft breasts. Laurie grew sleepy. She yawned and pulled her right pointer finger back up to her clitoris and crowned it with swift circles until she had released the pressure of the day and her vaginal muscles were contracting, her heart was pounding, and her blood was performing a victory lap in her vessels.

In high school, Laurie's friend Caite had told her that women have a finite number of orgasms available to them in their lives and most women who have had a lot of sex stop

22

having them once they get into their fifties or sixties, but sometimes as early as their forties. Laurie knew deep down from since hearing this factoid that it was one of the many pieces of bullshit that Caite would spread without ill intentions, yet Laurie still thought about it most times she had an orgasm. How many did she have left? Was that one worth it? She'd probably rate that one a six out of ten. It was good and efficient. Efficient wasn't always the goal, but this evening Laurie was content to roll over and fall asleep quickly.

Tricia was sobbing uncontrollably. She wore a form-fitting off-the-shoulders black dress with a wide-brimmed black hat and she wiped her tears with a black sequined handkerchief. Laurie recognized her face from photos. Today, however, she was wearing darker eyeliner, which smeared down her cheeks and her usual mulberry lipstick was replaced by a deeper color, more like a burgundy.

Though a missing person is usually not presumed dead before five years and an application for a death certificate, Matthew's body-less funeral was held at Radiant Greens County Club three weeks later. Radiant Greens had the best catering for weddings, retirement parties, and milestone birthdays, and once the largely-advertised coming out party of the owner's son who was not actually homosexual, but agreed to play along in order to make the club look more progressive. "We don't have a funeral menu, but I'm sure we could put something tougher for you," he told Tricia.

"Just as long as we can get the crab bites circulating at the beginning and finish with the mousse tartlets," Tricia explained. "We loved our son very much and he would have wanted his guests to find comfort in some nice food."

"Visitation" was from 4-6 pm, immediately followed by a "funeral." Laurie arrived at 5:50 pm and hoped she didn't see the few friends of Matthew's that she had ever met. Laurie and Matthew had been out a few months ago at The Sandy Duck, an outdoor bar with a beach-inspired sand floor and pastel Adirondack chairs placed in clunky groups. It was there that they had run into Mike and Nashae. Mike worked with Matthew every day and would surely have questions for her that she couldn't answer within earshot of Matthew's family. Fortunately for Laurie she didn't see Mike anywhere. The only people that Laurie recognized were from pictures that Matthew had shown to her. She thought maybe somebody would recognize her from a photo or two that Matthew had shown them, but nobody did.

Laurie walked down the walkway to the party pavilion where gorgeous floral arrangements of richly colored lilies and roses lined the perimeter. At the center of the pavilion was a bright and glossy white oversized casket covered with red roses and about a dozen over-worn stuffed animals, presumably childhood toys of Matthew's. Laurie thought about this. Wait. Why was there a casket if there wasn't a body to be found? Was there anything in there? Was there a placeholder for a body? How much does something like that cost? She suppressed her urge to knock on the casket and listen for a sound of either hollowness or occupancy.

Laurie's mind was racing. "It would be weird to greet Matthew's mother. It would be weird to not greet her. Which would be worse? How many people are here? It's not crowded enough to get away with not offering any words of sympathy." Laurie's nervous thoughts kept firing while she counted that there were 38 people in attendance. Laurie slowly made her way toward Tricia and waited for an opening in the conversation she was having with two other women in their 60s, one who was also wearing a black dress, and one who was wearing workout leggings, a crushed velour zipper hoodie, and tennis shoes. It looked like Tricia's friend on her left had stepped out of a senior citizen cruise commercial and her friend on her right had come directly from an exercise class.

There was a pause between the three of them after a cacophony of chortles, snorts, and throat laughing coming from Tricia's workout buddy, her dress-clad friend, and Tricia, respectively. Laurie cut in quickly. Time to get this over with so she could pay her respects and go home.

"I'm so sorry for your loss. I can't imagine what it must be like to lose your son. Thank you for having this gathering."

"And who are you? Did you work with Mattie? Or were you a teacher of his? Mrs. Lambone? Right? First grade? Or second? Sixth? I knew I remembered you." Tricia babbled, looking Laurie up and down.

"Oh no, I was a friend of his. I always enjoyed spending time with him."

"Oh."

"I'm Laurie."

Tricia blinked twice and then made an uncomfortable smile. Laurie looked into Tricia's face. She had clearly gone in for botulinum injectables a few days ago, but the face lifting chemicals hadn't had time to fully settle, so her facial muscles looked mildly swollen, like they were outlined with a web of dental floss that was holding her face together, like nylon netting encasing a whole bird of dead, refrigerated poultry. "What do you do, Laurie?" asked Tricia.

"Oh, I'm a realtor," Laurie told her.

"Oh! What a God-send! And you were a friend of Mattie's! I don't know any realtors but I need one now, sadly, to sell my son's condo." Tricia told Laurie. Tricia did in fact have a close friend who was a realtor but her current state of anger with every person who wasn't in attendance at Matthew's "funeral" was placed on her shit list and would have to knowingly or unknowingly work their way up from the bottom again, at least until Tricia forgot who was on which of her lists and in what ranking.

"I'd love to help you, Mrs.." Laurie began, waiting for Tricia to finish the sentence despite Laurie knowing very well her and Matthew's last name.

"Bellio. I'm Tricia Bellio."

"It's lovely to meet you Mrs. Bellio, but of course the circumstances are regretful. Again, I'm sorry. Here's my card and you can just call me whenever you're ready to think about selling that condo, but of course take your time. I'm sure you're not quite there yet." Laurie handed Tricia her realtor business card, yellow and silver diagonal stripes accentuating the Allington Liberty Group logo. Unlike many realtor business cards, Laurie's lacked a professional headshot. She didn't include a photo at all, which arguably made the card look more formal and professional, though it lacked approachability.

"I'll definitely give you a ring this week!" Tricia told Laurie. Laurie smiled and turned away, acting as if she were about to go mingle with Matthew's other friends, but she wasn't. Matthew hardly had any friends present and Laurie didn't really know any of the people there. The folks she did interact with seemed to be faux socialites from the country club who knew Tricia and were either there for the premium hors d'oeuvres or were afraid of the social consequences of choosing another engagement over this one.

The crab bites were delicious. Laurie grabbed two more without thinking as soon as she heard a man wearing a clerical collar loudly clear his throat and start heading toward the rollable podium near the cartoonish casket. She looked at the ground and headed for a folding chair in the back row.

"We are gathered to mourn the loss of Matthew Bellio, a

beautiful soul" the country club's rent-a-priest began, his hands making their way into the front pockets of his jeans. Laurie ate her two crab bites as quietly as she could. The sweat from her palms had softened the crispiness of the their fried exteriors. Oh no. Did her hands smell like crab now? She retrieved a tissue out of her purse very slowly, trying not to make any noise or call any attention to herself. She wiped her crabby mitts and then stuck the tissue back into her purse. An elderly gentleman in a suit two seats down from her began to cough abruptly, as if perhaps he had also just inhaled two crab bites and had accidentally aspirated a chunk of one of them. Laurie felt embarrassed even though she had nothing to do with the disruption. A few people turned around to see first the source of the noise and then if the man was okay. Tricia Bellio forced an audible scoff at the interruption and then immediately added a sob, remembering that she wanted to bring the room back to her own pain and didn't care to share any available empathy from the funeral's attendees.

"Harry, let's go get some water." the woman next to the coughing man said. She helped him stand up and she slowly escorted him inside the main building of the club. She looked about twenty years younger than he did. Laurie noticed their matching wedding bands and she wondered if he was completely loaded and she was just trying to hang on for a few more years before she'd inherit several strip malls or plentiful stock in a major corporation. Her mind followed the possible story of the older man and the younger woman up through his final days as she loaded his feeding tube and gave him sponge baths. She imagined the man dying while the woman cried one single tear, the most beautiful tear he ever saw, and then her taking a huge breath of relief after his last breath ever. She wondered where they had met. In her mind's story, she assumed they had met six years ago in this very country club. It's weird to think how some first meetings change your life completely and some don't seem to matter at all.

Laurie thought back to when she met Matthew.

It was March of 2012 and Laurie was bored. She had been out with various colleagues from the Allington Liberty group, Shay most often, but it wasn't like she felt she had friends she could count on. The bar scene was tired anyway.

The modern woman tracks down what she wants via the most efficient way possible: the Internet. Laurie slumped into her computer chair and opened her online dating profile. At this point in her life she had chosen to keep this section of herself very separate from her other business, so she had never installed the LoveHappens app on her phone and she had changed her account settings so that she would never receive notifications in her email concerning activity on the site. She felt this was healthiest. Very few women acknowledge the constant influx of photographed penises that quickly clog the inboxes of lady users. Laurie knew that it would never be wise to open up her LoveHappens account at work because anyone passing by would assume she had navigated to the array of dicks on her screen, rather than having been sent them. Opening up a dating site was a little bit like passing through an unattended farm stand in that Laurie would immediately be presented with an incredible number of phalli. At least she could admire the diversity. Various sizes, colors, shapes, and shades of squashes, eggplants, melons, cucumbers, yams, peaches, berries, onions, and peppers would appear on her screen. She always spent the first few minutes at the computer deleting pictures of cocks and blocking users, or rather, weeding the garden.

"You have 14 new matches." LoveHappens told her. She looked at them in grid view. Six of them had human profile pictures and the other eight displayed memes, flags, funny animals, or beer. Of the six humans, four of them had not bothered to add any information to their profiles other than the minimum requirements of gender, age, location, and "looking for." Laurie approved the two men who remained by clicking the smiley face in the bottom right corner of their profile pictures, meaning that if they had also clicked the smiley face on her profile picture, then they would receive a notification, usually worded along the lines of, "Laurie has sent a smile your way! Click here to say hello!"

Laurie wanted to go out tonight. She didn't want to exchange messages for two weeks and then talk about the idea of possibly meeting after an extensive phone call or two. She didn't want to get to know anybody's online persona. She wanted to have a drink with a human being within the next three hours. She opened the tab with her list of "Shared Smiles."

"Hey Chris! Would you like to go get a drink with me this evening?" Laurie typed quickly and sent. She waited a minute. The read status of the message changed from "unread" to "viewed." Another minute passed. No response. Laurie copy +pasted the same message into another message box, but she deleted the name Chris and typed in Brandon.

After Brandon's two minutes had expired, she threw out invitations to Matthew, Jason, Mark, and Eli. She got up from her computer chair, picked her cuter jeans up from her bedroom floor, shimmied into them, and began to look for a presentable shirt in her closet. There! The sound! And again! Two notifications from the site must mean she had two new messages. The first one was from Brandon: "Maybe tmrw?"

Laurie ignored Brandon's response and looked at the next message: "How's Breakers at 8:30?"

"Yes. I'd love to. I'll see you at Breakers at 8:30."

"Great!"

She'd be meeting Matthew. She hadn't thought their relationship would end with crab bites at an outdoor funeral, but at least she had finally gotten her meeting his mother over with.

The next morning at 7:33, Tricia's phone rang.

"Hello?" Laurie said, still half asleep.

"Is this Laurie?"

"Yes; this is Laurie. Good morning. How may I help you?"

"Well I talked with you yesterday. I met you at my son's funeral, which is so weird for me to say. Ha, well, I wanted to got ahead and get the ball rolling on selling that condo. Time is money, you know, I'm sure."

"Of course. Mrs. Bellio. When would be a convenient time for you to-"

"Can you meet me there today?" Tricia said, cutting Laurie off.

"Yes! What time work-"

"What time works for you?" Tricia interrupted again.

"I can be there as soon as-"

"Could you do ten o'clock this morning?"

"Yes." Laurie said quickly. "What's the address?"

"1801 W. Cary."

"Got it. Thank you; I'll see you there at ten."

"Okay- good-"

"Wait! What's the unit number?" Laurie had almost forgotten to ask for the unit number. She hoped she wouldn't make any other egregious blunders during the sale of this condo. It was going to be hard to ask all of the right questions.

"It's Unit 32."

"Excellent. Thank yo-"

Tricia hung up. Laurie immediately got out of bed and went to her purse to find her keys. She removed Matthew's condo key from her keyring and stuck it in the drawer of her jewelry box where she kept keys she no longer needed, a few of which she had completely forgotten what doors they unlocked.

Tricia arrived at 10:09 at Matthew's door, but did not acknowledge her tardiness. Today she was wearing white tapered pants and a black knit shirt with thin horizontal pink stripes. "Hellllo, Laurie," Tricia said, elongating her 'el' sound. Laurie was pretty sure she wasn't having a stroke, but she leaned forward a little bit to make sure Tricia's eyes looked okay, just in case. Tricia opened the door and went in first. "I think it's important that we discuss this sale in person so that I can point out some features of this condo that are particularly special. There are definitely some expensive upgrades that don't come standard and you probably wouldn't notice." Tricia said, gliding her hand through the air as if Laurie had never seen an apartment style condo before. "This sofa wasn't cheap."

"That looks like a very nice sofa, but statistically, home buyers are more likely to make a purchase if there are as few furnishings as possible. It helps them to imagine their things in the space and start to think about their potential ownership, rather than thinking of the space as belonging to somebody else. If you need help having furniture moved out or want me to make arrangements for a storage unit for you, I'd be happy to set up whatever you'd like. I can get a great deal; The Allington Liberty Group has some great business relationships, particularly in storage." Laurie explained. Tricia lowered her eyes and glared at the builder's grade carpet in Matthew's living room. Laurie lifted the conversation back up, saying, "We can talk all about how to best stage this home later. Would you like to show me the rest?"

"Mmmhmm." Hummed Tricia. "Here's the *master* bedroom."

"It's the *only* bedroom" Laurie thought to herself.

They walked into Matthew's bedroom, which still had most of Matthew's clothes in the closet and his blue flannel sheets were still the way that Laurie had last seen them. The fitted sheet was barely clinging to the pad-less mattress and the flat sheet was balled up and halfway under the bed. Matthew's favorite fleece blanket was covering his flattened pillow, which had more drool stains than a teething toddler's playpen. Tricia walked over to the bathroom door and turned on the light. "His and hers sinks. That's a pretty penny. Nice." Laurie nodded and smiled energetically, taking notes even though she didn't need to.

"And this way to the kitchen," Tricia said, as if they hadn't passed the kitchen on the way to the bedroom. "The kitchen has a lot of upgrades. Nice. The appliances are new." Laurie opened the refrigerator and looked at the label in the upper left corner.

"It looks like it's a 2005," Laurie said, writing down the year in her notebook, "and the stove, microwave, and dishwasher were part of the same package?" Tricia looked at Laurie with widening eyes. Her eyebrows lifted and her chin lowered. "Let me just check the years of those." Laurie wrote down the years of the appliances even though she was very aware that they were part of the same eight-year-old contractor's bundle.

Laurie heard Tricia's bony hand knock three times on inside of the stainless steel sink. "And this. I bet you've never seen a garbage disposal like this. It's a top-of-the-line. It's a *luuxxxury* garbage disposal." She said, really sinking into the word *luxury*, her featherbed of a word. "When Mattie moved in here I cooked him chicken parmigiana, and the original garbage disposal couldn't even handle the residue from our dinner plates." Laurie opened the cabinet below the sink and looked at the disposal underneath while recalling the incident that Tricia was referencing. Laurie remembered this incident. The material that strangled the original garbage disposal to its untimely end was in fact the trimmings of the chicken. Tricia, trying to remove any visible fat from the already boneless skinless chicken breasts had cut away the white tendons and wasted a sizable amount of meat in the process. Laurie knew all about this because she was the one who reached into the disposal and untangled the goopy mess from the disposal's grinder blades in order to properly throw it all away after the smell had gotten so bad that she couldn't stand it any more, which was three days after the dinner had been cooked. The scent of rotting meat hadn't seemed bother Matthew a bit.

"Wow!" Laurie said. "You're right; I've never used one of these. This looks really nice. I bet you could grind up anything in here."

Even though it took a few days for Laurie and Tricia to agree on a listing price, Matthew's condo went under contract within seven hours of its presale publishing. Usually when a contract was ratified for one of Laurie's listings she would take herself out to a celebratory dinner instead of going back to her townhome and scraping together various leftovers from her fridge or eating a patchwork of snacks like she did many evenings. Laurie wasn't sure what she wanted so she settled on a consistently tasty and nourishing Chesapeake Chicken from Bay Grille with garlic sautéed asparagus.

Three weeks later, Tricia Bellio and the Hernandez family signed the pile of forms and addendums, thus finalizing the sale of Matthew's condo. This meant it was time for Laurie to take herself out again. Laurie sat at the bar of Chisme and sipped her victorious margarita. Should she order tacos or arepas? After Laurie closed on a property, she usually took herself out for whatever sounded good to her. Two months ago when she closed on a small rancher, she took herself out for a rare ribeye, grilled broccoli, and a salty baked potato with a guava and passionfruit IPA. Tonight, she desired a large salt-rimmed margarita and some composition of fried corn, cheese, and slowly stewed meat.

Laurie knew people who weren't comfortable dining or drinking alone, but she had made a decision one evening a few years ago that she wouldn't let the possibility of judgment from strangers keep her from enjoying freshly prepared entrees and beverages instead of scooping them out of floppy styrofoam takeout containers and then eating them alone on her couch while the TV distracted her from the sogginess of tacos or arepas which had absorbed the condensation from their own steam and were no longer worth restaurant prices.

Laurie dipped a warm, salt-crusted chip in cold pureed salsa. The freshness of the lime, cilantro, and red onion made her close her eyes in pleasure for couple seconds as she crunched and swallowed. She had two more chips with as much salsa as she could fit onto them and then she sipped her water and pulled out her phone. She checked her email and then she toggled between two of her social media accounts. Her mouth was full of lime juice, tequila, and salt, but her heart felt empty. Even though she was willing to eat by herself in a restaurant, she wanted company. She wanted to laugh and smile and not have to work so hard to entertain herself. She checked her email again. Nothing. Whew. Nothing. Ugh. She swiped over to the App Store icon. Should she download it? What would be the harm? She had told herself she wouldn't put dating apps on her phone, partly because she didn't want to develop an obsession or dependence on them, but tonight she wanted to move forward. She took a quick look over her shoulder to make sure nobody had an eye on her phone before she hit download, as if it were porn she was hiding and not an algorithmic matchmaking tool.

Laurie marveled at LoveHappens. Twenty years ago, single people had to leave their couch in order to meet a person and set themselves up on a date. It must have been horrible. Laurie would gladly endure the filtering and deleting of the avalanche of dick pics that filled her inbox most days in order to appreciate the digital catalogue of men she could potentially meet. Each day, Laurie had a handful of new messages and notifications that somebody had liked one of her photos. Now that she had the application on her phone, it was like she had a pocket-sized tin filled with an endless supply of little dopamine-filled mints, so popable, so easy, so discreet, and so refreshing. She glided through the pictures of men with much more ease than the handful of times she had accessed the site through her phone's browser. As long as she ignored the scuzzy communication and accepted the compliments that came her way as genuine, she felt confident when she interacted with LoveHappens. Laurie had decided to order neither the tacos nor the arepas but the chile rellenos and they arrived so hot that she could hear the pressure of the juices trapped by the caramelized outer skin of the poblano peppers. Laurie loved poblano peppers. She also loved that the cook had included the drips of blended cheese which had hit the grill and bubbled, morphing into crispy, salty, golden-brown discs. She pressed the side of her fork into one of the peppers and hot cheese streamed out, like thick shampoo from an industrial salon pump. Laurie took tiny bites of the cheesy, peppery masterpiece on her plate and she scrolled through profiles of men on her phone. A profile should take ninety seconds to read, she decided. Anything longer than that belonged to someone too emotionally needy. It was too demanding. Anything shorter than twenty-five words, however, was too short and must belong to a person who is too inconsiderate to write more than two sentences. A man shouldn't be able to skate by on just a photo and the vaguest answers to profile prompt questions. Also, any man who responded "Just livin' life," to any of the prompt questions was immediately taken out of consideration for a date. She had passed on a few profiles, but then she saw a new notification. "Mark liked your photo." She always wondered which photo a man would choose to voice admiration for. Her profile photo, which was visible to all who visited her site was taken the same day that her professional head shot was taken for her realtor promotional materials. She was wearing professionally done make-up and the photo had been retouched by an artist so that her eyes were just slightly bigger, her smile was a little wider, the soft area under her chin was minimized, and the blemish and freckles on her upper chest were nonexistent. Which photo did Mark like? She viewed the number of hearts on her profile picture; it was still at twenty-seven. She scrolled though her other available photos and noticed that the full body shot of her at her cousin's picnic taken while she was leaning against an oak tree with the sun illuminating her hair had one more heart next to it. There were now six hearts where there had only been five a few minutes ago. Mark had liked her favorite photo of herself. She went to his profile and perused his pictures. It annoyed her that he was wearing sunglasses in most of his photographs. How was she supposed to see his eyes? For all she knew, maybe he was hiding the fact that he didn't have eyes at all. Maybe he had mis-matched glass eyes. Maybe he couldn't afford glass eyes and he had balled up socks shoved in his eye sockets instead of eyes. Maybe he had vertical slit-shaped pupils like a cat. Maybe his eyes were beautiful. Probably not. Mark's cutest photo was of him on a boat drinking a glass of wine. She thought she should return the compliment that he had given her, so she clicked the tiny heart icon in the bottom right corner of the photo.

Laurie set her phone face down on the table and placed her full attention back on her chile rellenos. She savored the dish and felt the two stuffed peppers were exactly the right flavor and quantity of food she had wanted. She always felt a little sad when she was served rice and beans with a meal but had hit a point where she knew she wouldn't feel very well for a few hours if she ate them. She felt weird about leaving them on her plate, weird about asking for a wasteful styrofoam container all for just some rice and beans, and weirdest of all about eating them anyway to avoid the previous two options. She was happy to have a flirtatious distraction and she didn't have to spend her remaining dinner time thinking about the rice and beans. While she waited for her check, she picked up her phone again. There was a message from Mark.

"Good evening, gorgeous. What are you up to?"

Chapter Two

Don't Talk to a Man First

April 2013

"Excuse me, are you Laurie?" Mark asked, his bright eyes reflecting most of the light available in Vintage 50, a reliable bar with a slightly older crowd. Mark's teeth were also bright, reminding Laurie of the sun's rays bouncing off of a lake's surface.

"I am." Laurie said, smiling slowly, something that she had practiced in the mirror many times but didn't actually do in public unless she was feeling comfortable and confident.

"Whatcha havin?" Mark asked as she took a large sip of her vodka soda. She was about to respond "It's a vodka soda," but a server appeared table-side and Mark ordered a whiskey on the rocks without pausing. "Man, you are looking very nice. I like your earrings and you have a very cute smile" he said, casually licking his lips. Mark was inquisitive in an upbeat way and he kept the conversation moving with prompts like, "Do you have any siblings?" and "Tell me about your job."

"And what do you do?" She asked him.

"Oh, this week I've been struggling with a big project but I'm happy to be wrapping things up. What's your favorite movie?" he said, bouncing quickly into a cue for her to speak again. She didn't have a favorite movie.

"You've Got Mail, probably." she said.

"What is that, like late 90s?" he asked.

"Yeah; I feel like that movie was the very beginning of online dating, so it feels relevant to me right now even though it's old. You've seen it?" she asked, tilting her head forward and her glass a little to the side.

"I think so. Tom Hanks…" he verified.

"Meg Ryan." she said joining in with him. He acknowledged the solid and satisfying feeling of saying the words in unison.

"As a realtor, what was the coolest property you ever showed?"

"Well there was this one doctor who had a helipad on top of the house and that was pretty cool. I stayed a few minutes after the showing and took the elevator up to explore. There was a lot of flat land around; I don't see why any incoming helicopters couldn't just land in the yard, but then again I don't really know anything about privately owned aircrafts. I showed the place to a client, but I knew he wasn't going to actually be interested. Plus there aren't really guidelines for realtors on how to assess the value of a helipad, so I heard the process was frustrating and messy for both agents. I didn't mind sitting that one out."

"So this doctor guy was pretty loaded."

"Yeah, *she* seemed very financially successful."

"Oh, *she*, wow."

"Would you like to have another round?" he asked.

"Okay, yes." Laurie said, settling into her chair a little more.

"I'm going to run to the restroom really quickly but if the server comes back I'd like another of the same."

"Got it." she said, nodding. When Mark returned from the bathroom, he pulled his chair over from the opposite side of their little square table where he was sitting across from her over to the side of the table in order to sit right next to her. Laurie hid a slightly startled reaction. She always thought it was weird when couples would sit in unnatural arrangements in restaurants and bars in order to be closer to each other. It felt like they were more trying to *show* that they were physically close to each other than actually enjoy the proximity. Laurie felt particularly grossed out when a couple would occupy the largest booth in a restaurant, but choose to sit on the same side. Not only would they have to crane their necks to the side in order to see their date's face, but they would be close enough to hear their partner's chewing noises during the meal. She wondered if people who engaged in same-side booth-sitting tried to order foods that were more quiet: mashed potatoes, but not slurpable soup. Pasta, but not crunchy salad. Shredded chicken, but not steak with prospects of gristle.

Strong, warm fingertips set into the tense hunk of muscle just above Laurie's left knee. She exhaled and waited. Mark's fingers glided in and out a few times before his palm sank down, sending a happy vibration up to her hips and out through her spine. When she turned her head toward him without a plan for any words, she found his face closer to hers than it was before. When did that happen? His hand massaging her leg felt powerful and relaxing, like she was somehow a yogi in a 100 degree room squeezing out her tension though a thousand sun salutations when he touched her that way.

They didn't say much. Their words came out slowly. They discussed models of cars whose designs they found most attractive and their assessments of local bars and restaurants they had been to in the past few months. They finished their third round and then Mark returned his massaging hand to his own sphere of personal space. "This place is going to close in under an hour. Would you like to come to my place and watch a movie? You know, no pressure. I know we just met; I'd just like to keep the good night going and get to know you a little more" he said with a sincere richness in his voice.

"Umm, I think we could probably do that. Where do you live? I mean, like, how far away?"

"I'm in Hilltop Estates. It's only fifteen minutes from here, twenty, tops." Mark raised his eyebrows at the bartender and nodded his head toward the door, which the bartender understood as a cue to bring them their check. The server who had brought them their drinks before must have clocked out around thirty minutes ago. Laurie pulled out her wallet and held it, making sure that he had visual evidence that she didn't expect him to pay for their drinks for whatever reason. Mark didn't acknowledge this with an, "I've got this" or "I'd like to pick up the check" but instead directly handed the bartender his credit card without looking at the printed itemization of their beverages. He kept his hand outstretched until the bartender had returned with his card twenty seconds later. Mark returned the card to his thin, chic wallet, which had far fewer contents than Laurie's wallet, jammed full of discount membership cards and clogged with old receipts. The two left Vintage 50 side by side. When the backs of their hands grazed in the parking lot, Mark reached around and interlaced his fingers with hers. He then brought their joined hands up to kiss the back of Laurie's hand. She let him bring her hand up and over his head, resting it at the back of his neck so he could wrap his arms around her waist and kiss her. His lips were like firm slices of ripe plums, sensual yet nurturing.

"Where's your car?" Mark asked her.

"Hmm? Oh, just one row over. It's right there." she said, needing a second to come out of her kiss-induced trance, realize that they wouldn't be driving together, find her Civic, and point it out to him. Mark walked with her to the car and opened the driver's side door for her after she unlocked it with the remote.

"So you'll follow me" he said. She nodded. "Bye, beautiful."

He walked back to his white 2013 Acura TL, waited for her to appear behind him at the exit of the bar's parking lot, and then they drove the speed limits to Mark's place.

The door opened smoothly and a fresh citrusy scent diminished her natural distrust. She entered the split-level home, following him. It was surprisingly clean. She could imagine living here in five years. If she lived here, she would never have to face the piles of clutter that seemed to accumulate around her. She would clean up immediately after every meal. She would never let a piece of junk mail enter the home; it would magically disappear at the door without her having to make any decisions about where to put it, whether or not the recycling center would accept it, or if she might need some of the information printed on it at some point later in her life. She would own exactly thirty perfect articles of clothing that would hang in her closet like a set of tubular bells, an ensemble. She would put the perfect outfit together each day without trying on different combinations. Her laundry hamper would never have rejected remainder pieces at the bottom of it because all of these perfect articles of clothing could be washed together with minimal effort. Her white camisoles that couldn't be washed with her black slacks would automatically disappear, possibly having never existed at all. She could be amazingly put-together in a home like this one and everybody would see her and think about how she was the model assembly of aesthetic and productivity.

She had thought his house would be dirtier. There might

be a pizza box in the kitchen, but no such evidence that this man ever ate anything inside this home existed.

"What can I get you to drink?"

She noticed the bar display between the two windows and chose her default beverage for the occasion.

"May I have a gin and tonic please?"

"I don't have tonic but let me get you a gin." He poured her three fingers of gin and also handed her a bottle of water.

"Thank you," she said, trying to catch his eyes and draw him into her for some connection. He sat on the couch while she sipped her gin in the entrance way. He patted his hand on the cushion beside him, summoning her to join him. As she did, she felt meltingly comforted by his arm around her, pulling her close to him, warmth building between their cuddling sides. His drinking glass made a pleasantly solid clank on the glass end table beside him as he abandoned it to play with her, first depositing her glass on the coffee table in front of them. Clank. Ah. His arm reached across and cradled the back of her skull. His fingers nestled into her hair like a crab descending into the sand. They locked eyes until their lips met and his strong, deep kiss relieved the tension in her lower back. Her face relaxed completely while his tongue massaged hers and he took playful gulps of her cheeks and jaw. The warm wetness migrated to her neck, just below her ear so the waves of gentle suction and tender pushing seemed amplified. His right leg swung over her and they traveled together, her reclining and him gathering atop her while his hands swiftly met behind her and unhooked her bra. She saw its simple black structure pooled in a sleeping heap on the floor, defeated. How had he removed her bra so smoothly without her even having removed her shirt? He kissed her again on the lips, like he was savoring a spoonful of bisque.

"Are you tired?" he whispered with concern as a night-shift

nurse might.

"Mmmhmm." She exhaled.

"Let's go to sleep."

"Okay" she said, happy for the invitation to skip an aggressive hour of sobering up before a cold and dark drive home on unfamiliar roads. He held her hand and stood up, the natural prompt for her to follow and they padded down the hall with light steps practically wagging their tails like a pair of playful puppies. His room was also a haven of clean lines and coordinated furnishings. He undressed, unbuttoning his crisp shirt, revealing toned pectorals through his tee, which came off too, uncovering animatedly defined biceps, triceps, and deltoids. His hands met at his belt buckle and part of her wanted to tear into his belt, button, and zipper, in order to free his dick. "Surely most cocks are unhappy to be enclosed in denim all day," she thought. Instead of helping, she pretended she wasn't trying to watch. She yawned and let her eyes droop, resting her head on the two rightmost pillows of the queen bed.

"Are you gonna fall asleep in jeans?" he asked.

"Mmmm no." She said, sliding them off under the sheets and letting them fall off of the side of the bed.

"Goodnight."

"Mmm Goodnight." She started falling into a comfortable sleep, breathing slowly, taking in the power of new attraction and feeling of social accomplishment. She wasn't at home in pajama pants eating leftover stir fry and scrolling through Instagram. She was out in the world experiencing what other young adults only wished for. She had put in the necessary work and vulnerability to meet somebody and go on a date like the ones in romantic comedies.

She woke up abruptly to his climbing onto her. His knees

sandwiched her thighs and his hands grasped the edges of her cotton underwear. His invasive thumbs under her butt felt misplaced, a rude mistake.

"Come on. You know you want it."

"Oh, no. I'm sleeping. I don't want to jump in right now. I feel like we just met. Because we did."

"Ugh." He looked to the side in annoyed disappointment. "Come on. You want it."

"No, I-"

"You want it. You're wet." He said, as he slid his finger under the crotch of her panties, and firmly inventoried her, counting: labia, clitoris, vaginal entrance. He yanked down her panties and pressed his hard cock against the opening of her warm canal. "Do you want me to wear a condom?" he asked.

"Yes. Wait! I don't think we should fuck tonigh-"

He grabbed a condom that he had placed to his left on the bed, tore the wrapper with his teeth, rolled it on, and pressed into her, announcing "Uhhhhhhhhh, so tight and hot," as if it were a generous compliment. He started thrusting deeply, his pubic bone bouncing on her pillowy body.

He came. He clobber-footed to the toilet and pissed an echoey stream, his non-dick clutching hand on the bathroom wall holding himself up. She rolled over and stared into the pores of the wall. Finally 6:30 came around, a great time to leave. At least she wouldn't have to drive home in the dark.

Laurie was tired, but not at all sleepy. She got back to her place around 7:15 on Saturday morning. She dropped her bag on the floor by the door, tossed her clothes and shoes into tiny mountains by her bed, put on sweatpants and a hoodie, and crawled onto her mattress, as if it were a life raft. She imagined herself drifting into a peaceful slumber, but it didn't happen. She imagined harder. She still failed at willing herself to sleep. She heard the familiar series of tones, signaling a cellular notification, so she tip-toed to her bag and dug out her phone. Oh thank god. A text message was waiting for her from Winston Smith, who was cancelling his appointment to see a condo across town this afternoon on account of a last-minute location change of his son's football game. Laurie let out an audible groan of relief. She didn't want to see anybody today. She didn't want to pretend that one condo was any more special than any other today. She didn't want to highlight breakfast nooks or proximity to jogging trails today. She didn't want to talk to anybody today.

Laurie went back to her room with silent steps and placed the phone on her nightstand. Even though the battery was at nine percent, she couldn't seem to find the energy to plug the charging cable into its port. She flopped back onto the bed and curled into a ball, hugging a pillow. She tried to sleep. Her eyes were closed, but she had never been more awake. She thought she could see the details of the insides of her eyelids and the stimulation was too much for her to drift off.

The notification tones of her phone rang out again. Was it Mark? Did she want him to call? Why in the world would she want that? She didn't want to date him. She didn't want to see him. She didn't want to think about him. Did she think he might be calling with some sort of apology? She wanted to pretend that he didn't exist and that last night she had stayed home and watched mindless television and eaten popcorn instead of going back to Mark's place? Why did she go? She knew it wasn't a good idea. She could have easily left the bar and gone straight home. She could have even left his house once she realized they weren't going to watch a movie. Laurie's back hurt from the built up anger and embarrassment growing in the muscle fibers of her shoulders. Why was she angry? Couldn't she just take a deep breath and pretend that this never happened? Thinking about Mark's intrusive penis wasn't going to help her get over her feelings, but she could still feel its jabbing her when she would shift and try to get comfortable.

Laurie's lack of sleeping success led her to take a hot shower. She grabbed her purple mesh bath puff, squirted layers of shower gel all over it, and squeezed it while turning it in her fists to create a thick lather. She rubbed herself all over but must have spent six or seven minutes scrubbing at her crotch trying to feel clean and fresh, rather than irritated and used. She let the hot water run over her and she zoned out while staring at the satisfyingly predictable lines of the tiles in the shower. Wait. Should she report him? Technically, shouldn't she? He had sex with her without her consent, despite her saying no, while she was under the influence of alcohol. There was a word for that situation but she was trying her hardest not to let it float into her mind. She wasn't a victim. She didn't want to carry around extra baggage. She didn't want to take the time to work it out. Isn't this something people go to therapy for? She didn't want to go to therapy. She didn't want to sit in a chair and talk to a stranger and pay an $80 copay for months when she could be doing other more enjoyable things and spending her money in ways she wanted.

What would even happen if she reported him? Was she just supposed to pick up her cell and call 911? Was she supposed to look up the non-emergency police number online? If she made some sort of call, wouldn't she have to go in for an examination and they would give her some sort of swab and test tube kit for her to stick up into herself and it would be kept in a giant refrigerator full of other test tubes full of DNA collected from other people's sensitive areas? Would she be interviewed? Would she get to decide whether or not she would press charges or was that up to the state of Maryland? Could she stop her mind from running loose with so many damn questions and just go the fuck to sleep?

She didn't know. Laurie finished her shower and returned

to her bed, but when she hit the mattress again, she couldn't remember whether or not she had used shampoo. She dozed off a few times for a few minutes in between bouts of assessing the imperfections in her bedroom ceiling.

When Laurie woke up it was Sunday. The sunlight peered in, beckoning for her to get up and get out of her townhome. Laurie's mouth felt sticky and gross; she felt the beginning of a layer of film that must have been building up on her tongue and inner cheeks since late Friday night. She brushed her teeth for three minutes while she walked around the house and straightened up messy areas. She gathered the clothes from her floor and started a load of laundry. She brewed an extra strong pot of coffee, even though she didn't intend to drink any hot coffee. When she was at home, she preferred an iced coffee made from leftover brewed coffee that she kept in a curvy glass carafe in her refrigerator. She wasn't out of leftover stored coffee, but the way the aroma of fresh coffee brewing filled her home made her feel energized, so she usually brewed coffee when she felt like she needed a fresh start or if she was about to have a guest over and she wanted that guest to think highly of her and her homemaking skills.

Laurie had two showings scheduled today. First she would meet with Steven and Clarissa, who were engaged and looking for their first home. They couldn't agree, however, if they wanted a townhouse or a single family home, so Laurie had been showing them options for both. Neither one of them looked like they knew their way around a lawnmower or a pair of hedge clippers, so she had been trying to steer them a little more toward a townhome. She had even shown them Matthew's condo, because they had expressed an interest in the location, but they told her when they toured it that it was "just too small for our growing family." Laurie wondered if Clarissa was pregnant. Obviously, she could never ask. She thought about how convenient a pregnancy would be in that condo given the

48

powder room's exquisite handling of hours of vomiting.

After Steven and Clarissa would see a townhouse not too far from her own at 11:00 am, she was actually going to see a property for herself. While she liked her townhouse a lot, sometimes she fantasized about having her own garden and a place where she could play music as loudly as she wanted without having to worry at all about neighbors being bothered. She didn't feel that she absolutely needed a garage, but she wanted a place where she wouldn't have to give guests extremely specific directions on where to find parking that wouldn't require a twenty minute walk and how to avoid finding that their car had been ticketed, or worse, towed away.

Laurie knew that any single-family property would have to have some significant flaw in order for her to be able to swoop in and afford it, even considering her not having to pay realtor fees and her having connections though her agency to contractors who did decent work. The last property she saw for herself was a short sale and the last owners had removed all of the toilets and plumbing fixtures, attempting to grab every last penny before the home was no longer theirs. "Easy." Laurie thought. Unfortunately, upon further investigation, it seemed that the previous owners had also managed to remove large sections of copper piping from the water lines. This would be much more expensive for Laurie to fix than she had been planning. Hopefully she would have better luck with today's showing.

Laurie found herself at the office on Monday morning around 9:30, delighted to put the weekend behind her. Allington Liberty's Chris Wexler and Shay Boggart were already there. "Did you have a good time with the in-laws last night?" Shay asked Chris as Laurie was entering.

"Bria's dad wouldn't shut up about Bria's ex boyfriend from high school. Apparently he ran into him in the grocery store and he just finished his bachelor's degree and for some reason we all needed to hear about it for a half an hour and then again periodically every twenty minutes after his fifth bourbon."

"But you've had your bachelor's for years, right?" Laurie asked reassuringly.

"Yeah. Every time I go over there though, Bria's dad feels like he needs to subtly tell Bria that she has better options than me and that she should practically do anything besides be with me. It's like, what would we do anyway? Get divorced and sell the house after Bria leaves me for her ex boyfriend and they live together in his parents' basement? Every time I see them I spend so much energy deflecting insults and fight-bait that I'm so tired and anxious the next day and I need serious recovery time."

"It'll get better; you'll figure out how to win over her parents." Shay said, while opening the email app on her phone and starting to respond to touring requests.

"No. I've tried so hard. Like I said, I'd be more likely to sell The Shit Hole than get along with Bria's folks" retorted Chris."

"Nobody will ever sell The Shit Hole," said Shay, hands on her hips. She smoothed out her white pencil skirt and then straightened the stacks of sample brochures and fliers.

"Hold on, what property have you deemed 'The Shit Hole?' What could possibly be so bad about that listing?" Laurie asked.

"I can't believe you haven't been dragged there. Consider yourself lucky. I've shown it four times. Last time I was there, one of the front porch steps cracked under a client." Shay said.

"When was this?" asked Laurie.

"Last month."

"It's been on the market a month?"

"Girl, it's been on the market a year. Anyway, that step cracking scared the shit out of her and she was a heavy lady and I had to pretend I didn't notice that the step broke so we didn't have to have a conversation about it. You know, if nobody acknowledges a the awkward-as-fuck situation and the embarrassment around it, can we all just move on? Like, if a tree falls in the woods and nobody is around to hear it, does it make a sound?" Shay barely took a breath when she spoke and she paced around, punctuating her points with the outstretching of her fingers, like she could spring into a jazz dance at any moment.

"Yeah, it makes a sound." Laurie responded softly.

Shay continued, "The Allington Liberty Group has collectively had 79 showings of that fucking house, more than the burned down crack den on 5th and Corduroy on its fourth price cut. Nobody has submitted an offer." Shay told Lisa. "I mean, they all figure, 'How bad can it be?' and then it always turns out when they look up how much it would cost to fix the drywall and the ceiling and the roof and the foundation and the grading issues and the pipes that it's not worth it and they'd be better off putting up the dough for a cookie-cutter, or really any other option out there at all."

"I see." said Laurie, nodding from the sofa. "Whose listing is it?"

"What it happens to be yours truly" said Chris.

"Woah; who owns it?" Laurie asked.

"That's the thing. I've never met her. Everything has been online. She had me list it over email and phone and I've never seen her."

"Weird," said Laurie, "that's so weird."

Just then, Laurie felt her phone vibrate in her pocket. She made sure that Shay and Chris weren't about to launch into any continuations of their rants before checking her showing requests. Laurie looked at the small screen. It wasn't a showing request. It was a text message. It was Mark. Her stomach sank. She opened the message and read, "We won't work out, sorry."

What? Laurie had never been broken up with by text message before. This wasn't a break up though; it's not like they were dating. They went on one date. Was it even a date? They had drinks together at a bar; was that a date? She learned that he was an asshole; was that a date? Laurie didn't know why she felt hot tears welling up in her eyes. She opened her eyelids more widely to try and dry them out. Her arms and legs felt heavy and her hair follicles began to stiffen and she could feel her individual hairs trying to escape her neatly tied ponytail. How dare he? Should she write back? What would she even say? Her phone suddenly felt dirty to her.

Laurie now tried looking up at the ceiling in order to keep tears from falling. When there was just too much liquid on the surfaces of her eyeballs, she abruptly got up and went into the restroom. Sometimes Laurie wished she worked in a company with a much bigger office with more than one individual bathroom. This was one of those times. She couldn't stay in here forever. She would have to deescalate her emotions as best as she could and then get out because somebody else would have to actually take a piss sooner or later. Laurie folded five squares of toilet paper into a small rectangle and ran some cool water over it. She held the wet toilet paper under her eyes, one at a time, trying to cool them down and preserve her carefully applied eyeliner. She thought of Friday night again and her hot tears shot out, falling into the sink. Wet toilet paper wasn't going to fix this. She looked in the mirror at the crying face, her eyes now much puffier than when she first attempted to calm them down. She tried taking a few deep breaths. This wasn't working. Whenever she would get to the top of a breath, her lungs would become unsteady again and give a short hiccup. Her trying to smooth out her breathing was only making it worse. She needed a distraction. She reached for her phone. Shit. Where was it? Oh no. She had left her phone in the couch back where Chris and Shay were probably talking about her and wondering why she was being such a weirdo, getting upset on a Monday morning and taking over the bathroom. Maybe she should just get her phone, grab her bag, and then leave early. That's exactly what she did. Laurie kept her head down as she retrieved her phone and her bag.

"I'm out" Laurie said to Chris and Shay as steadily as she could while walking toward the office exit. She didn't notice whether or not her colleagues responded as she tried to hold herself together without breaking down audibly.

Chapter Three

Be Mysterious

When Laurie got home she did what she usually did when she felt lost and needed direction. She focused herself by making a list in her notebook. It was usually a basic "to do" list, of activities that would make her feel focused like "go to the gym" and "restock vegetables." Sometimes she stared at the page when she felt like writing something like "don't kill anybody" until she could attempt to turn it into a positive statement like "do more yoga."

Laurie looked around her living room at the baskets of unfolded clean clothes. "I just have to get organized," she told herself. On the latest page of her notebook full of lists, "Don't let anybody rape you" somehow came out of her pen as "revamp laundry system." If she could just fix all of the little things in her life, the big pieces would have room to fall into place. Laurie remembered the time when a guest speaker visited her high school a few weeks before her graduation to present a lecture about time management. The man had a few large rocks, a small vat of pebbles, a bag of sand, and a glass of water. He challenged his audience to fit all of the materials into a beach bucket sitting on the table. Participants came up to the stage and manipulated the materials in various ways until the speaker made his point that the large rocks had to be placed in the bucket first and then the smaller materials should follow in order to most efficiently fill in the space. The large rocks apparently represented the most important values and their corresponding activities in life, like spending time with family or whatever, and the pebbles, sand, and water represented tiers of insignificant activities, presumably watching tv or texting mindlessly and whatnot. The speaker demonstrated that the big rocks had to be placed into the bucket first or else they wouldn't fit at all because the water, sand, and pebbles would form a gloopy obstruction at the bottom of the bucket and block the rocks from fitting in without toppling out of the top. Laurie still felt busy and flustered and she didn't see how this visual metaphor of the rocks, pebbles, sand, and water was supposed to help her now.

Where should she start in order to get her life back on track? Where did she go wrong? Staring at her notebook, her brain replayed the most drastic turn she figured her life had ever taken. She spent the next hour thinking about Luke.

Luke was charming. In Laurie's mind, Luke represented a vibrant era of collegiate fun, which now she remembered as being simple, sloppy, and full of poor attempts at sophistication. Laurie could remember their eyes first meeting in March of 2009 in Wonderland, a dive bar which had closed down permanently five or six months ago. He was cute, but she thought of their quick connection as an awkward mistake. Whoops. Unintended eye contact. Mildly embarrassing. Laurie's friends Vanessa, Gina, and Abby were out with her that night, which was one of many in a continuous celebration of completing their undergraduate degrees. They partied forth for the last month and a half remaining until graduation. The four alternated buying rounds of vodka sodas at the bar and then returning to the table where the other three were perched.

"Well ladies, I think I might be about ready to call it a night."

"Yeah," said Vanessa, grabbing her purse.

"Be right back- Gonna close my tab." Laurie called out. The other three couldn't hear her over the bassy remix that the DJ was playing but they figured she'd be back in a minute.

Laurie readied her credit card in her hand so she could quickly give it to the bartender whenever she caught her eye. Luke approached.

"Vodka sodas?" he asked Laurie. He held up his glass, indicating their newfound tiny commonality. Either he liked the taste of diluted vodka or he appreciated the unsweetened simplicity and value of the three dollar well drink. Laurie fit into the latter category.

The bartender held her hand out to accept Laurie's credit card. "Ready to close it out?" she asked.

"Yes. Thank you."

Luke took a step in closer to Laurie and told her, "Hey, well it looks like you're about to leave so I'll just man-up and ask you. May I have your phone number? I think you're really cute."

Laurie didn't want to seem like she had thought about this scenario too much. "Okay." She said. He handed her his phone with the new contact template brightly shining on the screen, the brightest light in the dingy establishment. She typed her name and cell number into the blanks and handed it back to him. Upon receiving his phone back, he immediately sent her a text. She hadn't even seen him typing, but there was the message on her phone. "Baby, it's Luke. You're beautiful and I want to kiss you."

Laurie signed the credit card receipt and then she let her hand fall into his. "You have my number." She said and she found herself back in step with Abby, Vanesssa, and Gina.

"Hi." Said Gina, addressing Luke's unexplained accompaniment as they all exited the bar to wait for the taxi that

Vanessa had called for them.

"This is Luke," Laurie proudly announced to her friends.

Abby's "It's nice to meet you" was friendly, but tired.

Laurie felt Luke slowly compress her hand, a clear request for her to look into his eyes. They faced each other on the sidewalk and he kissed her deeply. They each pulled back for a second to verify their instincts. Was she into this? Did he do this every night with whatever girl he found at the bar? Their eye contact seemed so naturally connective. He exhaled a heavy breath onto her neck as his cheek brushed her jawline; the humid air from his lungs felt like he was claiming her. She let out a soft sigh, a kittenesque sound of joyous vulnerability. This time she went in for the kiss. Her playful tongue touched his and she hugged him. His hands glided around to the small of her back and the other people waiting for their 1:30 am taxis seemed to blur together and then fade away. Luke guided Laurie a few steps away from her buddies who were in the brightest sphere of the streetlight. He gently pressed her up against the brick building exterior and they tried to melt into each other.

"Taxi's here, Laurie," Vanessa said loudly in the manner that one might throw a shoe into a room with a rat infestation, giving the rats enough time to scatter before a human entered, interrupting.

"I'll see you later." Luke said.

"Okay!" Laurie told him.

The ride home in the cab was a proud one.

When graduation rolled around, Laurie still wasn't sure what she wanted to do with her life in the sense of her career. She had explored teaching as a profession during college but had ultimately decided that it wasn't for her. If she changed her mind, however, she could apply for a teaching license fairly easily because she had all of the coursework under her belt. She hadn't really known which courses to take because she just didn't have a clear vision of what she wanted to do. She *did* know that she wanted to own a home as soon as she could manage it.

Laurie started looking at condos about a month before college graduation. Wasn't that the first priority? Didn't she need somewhere to live after graduating and moving off campus? She found a beautiful place that she loved and the mortgage would be less than any rentable apartment in the area, but unfortunately nobody had told her before she began researching locations that she couldn't finance a home purchase without a steady job. It didn't make any sense. How come it cost a ridiculous amount of money every month to not have been able to afford to pay for a home up front in cash, something that only very wealthy people could do? She felt angry every time she thought about how much time she had wasted finding the perfect condominium building to live in and going through way too much of the purchasing process before learning that it just wasn't a possibility for her at that time. Laurie had toured a fantastic place for sale, decided to make an offer, put down an earnest money deposit, but had to terminate her contract because she couldn't secure financing. Going through the process of making an offer on a home made her realize something though. Laurie wanted to be a realtor. She had decided this after her first tour of a condo she was considering right before graduation. Her reasoning was mostly a path-of-least-resistance scenario. She wanted to be a realtor for three reasons: she couldn't think of something she would rather do, she was pretty sure she could study and pass the Maryland Real Estate exam in less than a week, and she was certain that she never wanted to pay commission to another realtor when she was finally able to make a transaction.

Laurie winced as she signed her name on the application for a six month lease of the shittiest apartment around. It was okay; it was temporary. She would move into an apartment after her final exams and graduation and then immediately focus on the realtor licensing process and then job-hunting. Seven-hundred dollars a month would get her a studio apartment with peeling paint and a running toilet. She accepted that in the only unit available, there was a rectangular indentation spotted with damp mold in the carpet where the previous tenant had kept a large chest freezer packed full of wholesale fish. All 650 square feet of the apartment smelled like the dumpster behind a seafood market.

Unfortunately, Laurie's application to abide in the crumbling fish palace was rejected for the same reason that she couldn't nail down a mortgage: she didn't have a full time job. Shit. Laurie now had three weeks remaining until graduation, so it was time to buckle down and get the next chapter of her life in order. Laurie went to her last college classes, but she wasn't focused. She had always been quick to participate in academic discussions, but now her attention during them was completely on her notes for her real estate license. She cancelled her plans to attend an iconic senior year "fire and ice" party and she studied hard instead so that she could be ready for the first available real estate examination session on Saturday at a testing center she had never heard of. "God, this is pricey" she thought as she swiped her credit card for the $44 testing center fee. She would also have to cough up the $90 application fee due to the state of Maryland. "It would have been so much cheaper to down flaming shots followed by freezing cold shots rolling down from the frat-crafted ice luge while my best friends cheer me on."

Laurie made a list of every brokerage she could apply to work with. When she began to receive negative responses concerning her lack of experience, she considered going into business for herself. Ultimately, she decided against a leap into entrepreneurship mostly due to her fear of legal liability, but also because she didn't see herself selling houses forever. She thought she'd be touring clients around for maybe two years, four years tops, but here she was, about to slide into her sixth year and she didn't have an inkling of a next chapter. Sometimes she imagined flipping homes, but she lacked the capital. Deep down, she also knew she would suffer from boredom eventually. The first two homes she'd flip would be exciting, but by the third, she would be dreading the insignificant decisions. Ugh. Cabinets. Flooring again.

"Some day, I'm going to be super rich." Luke told Laurie periodically. "Other people are content with working predictable jobs for the entirety of their lives, but not me. I want to do something more. I want to make my own products. I want to be my own boss. I don't want to work to get somebody else rich; I want to work for myself. That would be the life. I could just go work in Hawaii for two months, brainstorming ideas. I could set my own hours and do whatever I wanted."

"Yeah, that would be a great way to live," said Laurie. "It's just that you'd have to make a lot of money in order to afford health insurance and have a little security."

"Well, yeah. I would."

"Sounds like you've got a vision for what you want. How would you get Hawaii-rich?" she asked.

"I would make so much money"Luke answered, annoyed at having to repeat himself.

Laurie took a breath and rephrased, "What would you do specifically that would earn you this enormous fortune you're talking about?"

"Well I'd build things."

Laurie waited for elaboration, which didn't come. She prodded on, "What are some of the products you would build?"

"Oh, anything. Anything that people need."

"What do people need?"

"There are so many things. We just have to brainstorm. I want to be able to live in a nice house by the water. Like, it doesn't have to be huge, but I want to live on a lake so I can go out in the morning with a coffee and look out on the water and just be, relaxed, you know?"

"Yeah. It would be nice to live by a lake. Most people don't get to do that."

"You wanna go get tacos?"

"Yes. Yes, I would like to go get tacos." Laurie said, smiling.

When Laurie had graduated from college, she had just barely met her goal of landing a job and place to live. Even though she had passed her realtor license examination on the first try, finding a firm or agency who could provide her with an actual job offer letter stating estimated income in writing proved difficult. She needed this in order to secure an apartment, as she didn't have pay stubs from full-time work that she could provide to prove that she could make enough money to pay her rent. The morning of her graduation ceremony, she interviewed with Allington Liberty Group. To her amazement, the interview flowed exceptionally well and they offered her a position by 11:00 am, a mere three hours before the University's commencement ceremony.

Looking back on the end of college, Laurie wished she had relished the last month of her collegiate days with the best friends she had ever had. Instead, she had poured almost all of her limited interpersonal energy into Luke, who quickly became her first boyfriend. Luke was five years older than Laurie and she loved going places with him because she felt sophisticated, as if she had blossomed into a crimson stargazer lily. The novelty of going to bars and legally ordering alcoholic beverages hadn't worn off yet and she was happy to peruse the menu and pick an eleven dollar cocktail with a gimmicky name. Laurie loved making out with him and showing off that she had somebody who wanted to be with her. She liked when he would hold her hand in public.

She never felt more alive than the first half of Tuesday evening in April of 2009 when they had split a bottle of shiraz at dinner and then decided to have a drink on the rooftop bar of a hotel. As they were riding the elevator up to its highest destination, atop the eighteenth floor, Laurie grabbed Luke's face and kissed him firmly. Luke immediately hit the elevator button for the next floor, number nine, but the hotel's security features prohibited the door from opening for them without first swiping a room key card. Luckily for them, two walker-adorned octogenarians were waiting on the twelfth floor to board the elevator. Luke gripped Laurie's hand when the elevator dinged and he stepped out on the twelfth floor, barely avoiding trampling the elderly couple. In an attempt to regain an image of politeness, he held his other arm over the elevator door while the surprised couple inched into the elevator. Laurie thought Luke was going to explode when the old women got the back leg of her walker wedged in the elevator door's crevice. Luke smiled and gripped the walker, pulling up and rescuing it from being crushed. As soon as the couple was safely boarded, Luke bolted down the hallway of the twelfth floor with Laurie right behind. What was he doing? They saw a line of light coming from a supply room with its door ajar. He pawed it open with one swipe, like a cat, and after verifying that it was unoccupied, he pulled Laurie into it and closed the door. His mouth enveloped hers. She forgot how to breathe as his hands went straight under her dress and tore down her underwear. He backed her onto a laundry folding table and accessed his hard cock with his right hand, freeing it from his zipper and boxers in one motion while he grasped a fist full of her right buttock with his left hand. He was inside her like lightening and she could feel the hot ridge of his dick's head rubbing every part of her inside. His blunt tip rammed the back wall of her vagina over and over until she thought she might scream from pleasure. Her delicate nerve endings were tantalized in a fantastic way, but then the scream came from Luke instead of her as he finished, pulling out and sending semen dripping onto the cement floor.

"That was amazing, babe," said Luke, "but I want to find a drink to keep this buzz going." He started grabbing and pulling boxes and bins off of the storage shelves, haphazardly shoving everything around like he was four years old and rummaging though a toy chest for his favorite fire truck. Some sample-sized shampoos fell out of a box and he kicked them under the steel shelving. "Finally!" he scoffed, tearing the packing tape off a cardboard shipment of tiny bottles of vodka, destined for mini bars. Like a machine, he a unscrewed a bottle, sent the liquid down his throat, and dropped the cap and empty vessel onto the floor until there were four bottles and four caps wading in the pile of watery splooge he had just released. Laurie felt sorry for the member of the cleaning staff who would find the mess and have to unstick the bottles from their cummy prison on the floor.

After Laurie pulled up her underwear and straightened her dress out, she and Luke headed back toward the elevator. When Luke pressed the down button at the elevator, she reminded him, "Oh, we were gonna go get that drink on the rooftop bar."

"Nah, I'm good now. We can head home."

"Oh, okay" she said, her dissatisfaction reverberating off of the shiny metal doors.

"Cool, I'm pretty tired" he said.

Not all of Laurie's days with Luke were as much of let-down as the time they had sex in the hotel supply closet. She had several fond memories of Luke and he had some great qualities that she thought were important aspects of a good partner.

For example, Luke was a really good swimmer and he loved spending time on the water. He and Laurie had gone swimming a handful of times, a few of which had ended in romantic moments in the water. She remembered one time that he rented a rowboat, packed a picnic, and led the way out to watch the sun's rays dance on the calm lake and feed her strawberries and wine.

"You seem really calm and pleasant." she told him, leaning on his shoulder.

"I feel that way when I'm with you." Luke told her in soft and low tones directly into her ear. The vibrations of his voice and his kind words made her release a delightful giggle.

"Also, I took two Xanax before I rented the boat. I wanted to take you on the water, but boats make me a little nervous sometimes." he told her.

"Oh. Um, are you okay? Like, how often do you do that?" She asked him, trying not to ruin the nice time they were having, but still looking for a way to reduce her concern.

"Oh, I don't take two every day."

"Do you... take *one* every day?"

"Usually."

"Oh. Is that... safe?"

"Mmmhmm; it's fine." Luke said, lying down in the rowboat.

"And do you often drink when you do that?"

"It makes it even more relaxing. It's good to relax. I get so stressed sometimes and I have to have good ways to calm down." Luke said, his words growing softer and more mumbly. They floated along in silence for a few minutes. The sun was still soft shoeing back and forth along the water and Laurie could hear several birds gossiping as the boat drifted past their trees.

Luke let out a low, wheezy breath, which Laurie ignored, until she heard another one just like it, and then another. His faint snoring grew louder and louder. Laurie wouldn't have minded a nap herself, but when she looked around, she didn't recognize anything.

"Hey, Luke?" Laurie asked with feigned cheeriness. There was no response except for rhythmic snoring.

"Luke." she said more loudly. Still nothing.

"Luke!" Laurie projected her voice, interrupting the birds and a nearby beaver. A growl escaped Luke's throat, the result of throat muscles flapping in toward each other instead of holding their shape. Laurie's embarrassment of the noise almost wanted to assure the wildlife around her that she wasn't the one making the terribly throaty snoring sounds. "Luke! Wake up! Do you know where we are?" She placed a hand on his shoulder and shook him, to no effect. Laurie looked around at the passing trees, their branches waving her on toward who knows where. They were far southwest of the trails and recreational spot that Laurie knew well. As they drifted down the Potomac River, the boat started picking up speed. The trees zipped by faster and the birds' conversations became more curt and succinct.

"Luke!" she tried again. His snoring inhalation was even louder, as if he was responding to her subconsciously in a completely useless manor. Laurie grabbed the oars and started rowing furiously against the current. She didn't know where their destination was. Did they even have one? Luke had said that he would arrange their river outing, but he didn't tell her where the rowboat portion would begin and end. While she rowed with all of her strength, the boat stayed stationary as the water raced under them. How long had she been rowing? It had been about thirty-five seconds. She should keep going, right? When her shoulders and back tensed up, she stopped and let the boat lurch down. Shit. Did they miss an obvious boat ramp? Were boat ramps obvious from the river? Were they even supposed to get out of the river at a ramp or were they just supposed to pull off to the side and bring the rowboat onto some muddy grass. Laurie couldn't remember the name of the shack where Luke had rented the boat. She would have searched on her phone for a return location for rowboats, but either all of her search terms were too broad or the information wasn't even published online. She couldn't find anything helpful. Her frantic internet search on her phone provided nothing helpful, just broad images of more distance down the unpredictable river.

Luke's snoring continued and developed a multilayered echo against the aluminum sides of the rowboat. Laurie tried to breathe calmly so that she wouldn't panic, but the grizzly sounds powered by Luke's lungs kept her from re-centering herself and thinking clearly. Fuck. Fuck. What to do. When she looked up, it seemed that the river was about to widen considerably. When she squinted, it seemed there was a grove ahead in the middle of the river. Trees. They were getting larger and marking a land mass ahead. Great! Wait. Something that looked like a small island was splitting the river into two branches and she would need to figure out which one of them to take. Maybe it didn't matter, but then again maybe it did. Maybe there was a dock or something on one side of the river where their journey was supposed to end.

"Luuuuuke!"

There was still no answer from the napping heap of wine and benzodiazepine. Laurie hated forced decisions, but she was going to have to either pick a branch of the river or land, quite possibly crashing the boat into the wild-looking island in the middle. Laurie's instinct was to veer to the right to exit the river, as if she were driving a car and wanted to leave the interstate in the most common way. However, when she thought about it, she tried to imagine a map of the Potomac River with Maryland to the north and Virginia to the south. Was Luke's plan to take them to Virginia? She really didn't think he had planned for the next portion of their outing to be in another state, so she started to use the oars to steer to the left. She watched the island begin and get wider and wider for four or five minutes and she wondered if she had made a good decision.

"Thad, grab me a brew!" Laurie thought she heard.

"Yah, where's the cooler?" another voice responded. Laurie looked around and hoped desperately to find the sources of the voices. She then heard the unmistakable honk of a pickup truck's horn that couldn't be far away. There must be a water access point or at least a picnic area around not too far. She examined the shoreline hard. She steered about forty feet away from the edge, wanting to be close enough to land the boat, but far enough to not risk getting stuck in shallow water. The hill banking the water seemed pretty steep and she didn't know if she could climb its rocky, muddy side, particularly in her sun dress and flip flops. Her bathing suit she wore underneath was now sweaty and sticking to her with uncomfortable heat. She wanted a glass of water so badly. She waited with eyes peeled for a good place to land, figuring she'd do her best and she probably wouldn't die. Sure enough, a brown strip appeared ahead. There was a water access point, a gradual dirt path cut out of the trees and hillside. She could land the boat there and then go find help. She steered as best as she could until the scraping thunk of the boat hitting the sandy bottom made her gasp with relief. She took off her yellow flip flops and tossed them to the front of the rowboat and carefully stepped out into the cold water. Her feet sunk into a slimy clay, but she grabbed the rope at the front of the boat and kept taking small steps toward the path, keeping her hips square as to not lose her balance while pulling the weight of Luke and his stupid boat along with her. Laurie was able to pull the rowboat halfway out of the water, but couldn't bring Luke any higher on the path when faced with the rocky friction of the dirt ramp.

The snoring stopped. This lightened Laurie's headache that she had only now realized that she had.

"Where are we?" Luke asked her, as if only a few seconds had passed since they last spoke.

"I don't know." Laurie said, taking a deep breath.

"Could you check?"

"No. I have never been on a rowboat and I don't know where we are and I stressed out pretty badly because when you fell asleep I thought I was going to get lost on the river and die, smattered against rocks and eaten by leeches." Laurie said quietly and sharply, over-articulating her consonant sounds, suppressing rage.

"That's ridiculous. Leeches live in stagnant water. They would never be found out here in the running water. Maybe some in the swampland close by, but not the actual river." Luke looked at Laurie and continued, "You look mad. What's up?"

"You fell asleep and I couldn't wake you up and I didn't know where we were going and I didn't know if we were safe or not, so I had to row this boat and pick a place to pull off. Where were we supposed to land? Did we pass it? Or did we have more time?"

"I don't know. Lemme find out." Luke pulled his phone out of his pocket and conducted the same fruitless internet search as Laurie had done before. "Gosh, you're sunburned."

Laurie put her fingers to her inflamed face and felt her torched skin. She would have cried but she was too dehydrated and her body was recirculating the water that she normally would have had available for tears. Her face, shoulders, chest, and arms were cooked lobster-red. She worried that she must look like Ronald McDonald's frumpy cousin in her yellow sundress with bright red skin. She looked down to see that somehow her legs were still very pale.

"I'm hungry. Do you want to go get dinner?" Luke asked, rubbing his stomach.

"Well, yes. Yes, I would like to go get dinner. How in the world do we get this boat back to wherever it needs to go?" Laurie said slowly, thinking Luke might not understand what is supposed to happen after you rent a boat.

"We can get it tomorrow. Let's walk up and see where we are and then we can call an Uber or something to take us to the car and then we can drive and get dinner. Mexican? I'm feeling like Mexican. Enchiladas. Maybe taquitos. Maybe both!" Luke told her, gaining excitement. Laurie didn't know how much money you get charged if you abandon a rowboat, but she was so happy that she hadn't put down her credit card.

"I'll get an Uber." she said.

Luke was Laurie's first committed boyfriend. Sometimes when she thought about him, she still experienced the magical feeling of being adored. She remembered how it made her feel when he expressed affection and how she had loved the excitement of his calling and texting her, them meeting up for dates, and her feeling like she could have sex whenever she wanted to. There must have been times when it was great, however, she found herself seemingly only remembering the encounters that were less than ideal. Their last Friday night date progressed without significance to Laurie until the credits of a horror film they had decided to see on a whim began rolling.

"Wanna go home?" he asked her. Laurie was little caught off guard, her feet sticking to the tile floor, layered with the soda and popcorn of viewers past.

"Yes please." She said, smiling and gazing into his dark eyes. Laurie usually liked to stay and watch the credits of a movie.

She felt like she somehow owed the artists a little recognition and that they at least deserved for her to watch their names scroll by in the darkness. The ushers crowding in the theater's corner, brooms and dustpans in hand, would often start to eye her if the other film patrons had already left and she was the last one keeping them from swooping in and minimally cleaning. This time, however, Laurie abandoned her inclination to watch the credits and she held Luke's hand as they ran off toward the parking lot. He opened the passenger side door of his purple Ford Mustang for her. "Thank you!"

"You're very welcome, my very attractive lady friend."

"I love that you have a purple car. It's so unique." Laurie told Luke.

"It's not purple. It's blue." he retorted, defense in his voice.

"Oh, well I guess it's little hard to tell in the dark."

The evening's summer breeze had cooled them through the open windows of Luke's purple sports car and carried the catchy song on the radio playing for the thousandth time that day back out onto the interstate. Laurie loved the ride all the way home, concluding as he parked at his townhouse, which was a very similar layout to the one she ended up buying a year later. For the time being, Luke's place felt sophisticated. He held the door to the townhome open for her. She might as well have been a princess in a fairy tale.

When Luke shut the door behind them, he kissed Laurie deeply. She kissed him back and thought about how to tantalize him throughout the upcoming foreplay. She specifically thought about how to use the staircase leading to the bedroom to her advantage.

"Hold on just a minute; I want to use the restroom first." Laurie whispered, trying to make the bathroom sound sexy. Luke guided Laurie, still kissing her, and leaned her against the back of his sofa. He reached under her dress and grabbed the soggy aisle of her underwear like he was clutching the strings of ninety balloons, yanked it toward her left side. His very erect penis pushed into her.

"Ow! Goddamit! What the fuck?" he shouted angrily, like an overbearing coach training an apprehensive child diver.

"Oh no! Shit. I'm sorry; you should have given me a minute. I needed to take that out."

"What the fuck is *it*?"

"Diva Cup."

He looked at her, his face muscles contorted, possibly permanently spelling offended.

"It's a menstrual cup. I told you; I needed to go to the bathroom first to take it out. If you had just waited a minute-"

"What the fuck is it doing in there?"

"A menstrual cup catches period blood. So you can empty it into the toilet. And not bleed everywhere. Once a month. Because women do that."

He stumbled into the bathroom without comment, his hand on his dick. She hoped she hadn't inadvertently damaged his equipment.

"Sorry!" she yelled toward the bathroom. Luke urinated loudly and then went to the kitchen to pour himself a glass of whiskey. "Hey, are you okay? I imagine that might have really hurt, like if the silicone stem went up you a little, like, a surprise catheter. Anyway, sorry."

Luke didn't acknowledge her apology. She thought she had sounded genuine, even though she wasn't sorry. She felt annoyed that he didn't listen her, particularly concerning important safety information regarding his penis in this case.

Laurie slept lightly in Luke's bed until the sun rose. When light flooded the room with its yellow morning glow, she looked over at Luke, facing away from her, his hair resting on the pillow like a curled up muskrat. She began the slow-motion dance of trying to leave without having to have a conversation. She wanted some time to herself in her own living space and she felt like she needed it as soon as possible. Laurie peeled back the comforter and put her feet down gradually, the balls of her feet making contact with the hard wood floor first. She grabbed her purse from the bedside table and stepped into the sloppy denim pile on the floor, her jeans from last night that she hadn't bothered to fold.

"Hey. Why are you going? I thought we were going to spend the weekend together." Luke asked. Laurie was shocked that he woke up.

"I kinda wanted to go home and get a few things done."

Luke stared at Laurie blankly. There was a long pause before he responded, "Oh."

Laurie continued gathering her things.

"Do you know if Lyme disease can go away on its own?"

"What?" Laurie asked. She searched for a connection to the situation but there was nothing.

"What do you want to get for dinner?"

"I don't know. Do you want to do dinner tonight?"

"Yeah!" Luke smiled. The puppy-like excitement in Luke's voice melted Laurie a little.

"You could pick up Mexcian. Enchiladas for me. Probably tacos for you. You could come back here and we could watch a movie and cuddle."

Laurie's annoyance drifted and she took a deep breath. She

smiled. "I'd like that." she told him. Luke put his arms behind his head, fingers laced, leaving his arm pit hairs to stretch and dance in the open air.

Laurie was already thinking about which restaurant would be the best option for picking up food on her way back to Luke's place. The enchiladas were better at Las Flores but the tacos were crispier and more flavorful at Señor Verde because they grilled their tortillas rather than just warming them. As Laurie got into her car to go home for a few hours, she remembered the time that Luke had commented on the difference in the enchiladas. He said once while eating the enchiladas from Señor Verde's, "The sauce has a little bit of a wet dog flavor to it." Laurie decided to go with Las Flores before her brain moved on to thinking about the most efficient route to take and at what time she should place the order so that the food would be as fresh and hot as possible. Laurie would place the order between 5:10 and 5:15, arrive at the restaurant by 5:30 having completed all other necessary errands first, and arrive back at Luke's place at 5:50. It was earlier than their preferred dinner time, but at least their food would be at peak deliciousness because the dinner rush wouldn't have started yet. Food was never quite as good if made during the dinner rush and it had more opportunity to sit out after its preparation, especially if there was a considerable line at the hosting podium where to-go orders were picked up.

When Laurie returned to Luke's place she was carrying six bags. One contained their favorite Mexican beer. One had Luke's favorite tequila. One had five limes from the grocery store, one had their hot food, and the other two bags were Laurie's purse and tote bag.

Luke greeted Laurie with a hug and a kiss on the cheek. He relieved her of the beer and the tequila, grabbing them both with tight fists and taking them from the entryway to his kitchen. He placed both in the center of his kitchen table. Laurie heard two exciting 'pops' as Luke removed two beers from the pack and opened them with his keychain bottle opener, which he usually carried in his right front pocket. Luke took a long swig of one of the beers and returned to Laurie, who was still in the entryway struggling with the groceries, her personal items, and their dinner entrees. Luke thrust out his right hand, delivering Laurie a beer. She smiled and waddled to the kitchen with the four bags she was still holding. Luke followed her, his arm still outstretched. Because the beer and tequila were occupying the kitchen table, she gently released her cargo onto the floor, sighed, and put the beer and tequila in Luke's refrigerator in order to clear the table for their enchiladas and tacos. Laurie neatly folded the paper bags from the liquor store and set them on the kitchen counter. She immediately changed her mind, picked them back up, folded them together into a smaller rectangle, and slid them into her tote bag. Now that her hands were free, Luke said, "here" and put the beer from his right hand into Laurie's left hand. When she set it on the table so that she could lift their dinner from the floor, she noticed that Luke had given her the bottle that he had already started drinking. Though hers was only half full, she decided not to say anything. She thought about making a joke about being an optimist or a pessimist concerning the halfway full or empty bottle, but she just smiled as she placed the warm bag from Las Flores on the table. Luke stumbled.

"Are you okay?" Laurie asked.

"Yeah, why?"

"You stumbled."

"No I didn't."

"Okay, fine" Laurie said, consciously repressing an eye roll. Luke took a step backward and planted his feet shoulder width apart on the kitchen floor. He took a long pull of his beer, finishing it in two large gulps. The empty bottle made a loud clank as he plopped it on the table next to the tacos Laurie was uncovering. Luke started to tilt backwards and then took three quick steps to steady himself. Laurie looked at Luke, thinking he might offer an explanation. When he didn't, she asked, "Did you start drinking before I got here?"

"No." He let out a thick and bubbly burp. Laurie's face soured as she exhaled for three seconds longer than she would have naturally. She was avoiding getting a whiff of Luke's burp. Its deep resonance as it surfaced could only mean a foul release of smelly stomach gas. Gross. Luke looked around the kitchen, whipping his head to the left and then the right, scanning the countertops. "Where'd the beers go?"

"The beer is in the fridge" Laurie told him. Luke lumbered toward the refrigerator like a heavy robot clomping through hot sand. Laurie finished laying out the food and she added the limes to the table. She removed her tote bag and purse from the kitchen floor and put them near the sofa in Luke's living room. When Laurie returned to the kitchen, Luke was popping open another beer. He turned from the refrigerator to see Laurie, the refrigerator door still hanging open. Luke flopped the back of his t-shirt back up and down, like a fan, the cool air from the fridge flowing onto Luke's sweaty back. Luke leaned forward a little bit and then steadied himself, his left hand grasping the open refrigerator door for support. His right arm relaxed and his hand tilted, sending a large splash of beer to the floor. Luke didn't react. "You spilled your beer" Laurie told him without emotion.

"No I didn't."

"Look." Laurie pointed to the floor.

Luke reached, grabbing and ripping the last paper towel from the roll that was sitting on the counter next to the fridge. The empty cardboard tube clumsily rocked back and forth, its streaks of bleached fibers on the roll's adhesive making Laurie imagine that the gluey bits of paper towel were stacks of teeter-totters, teetering and tottering in unison. Luke bent at the waist, folding halfway in order to clean up the mess, still standing in front of the open refrigerator. Luke exhaled and let his arms relax, dragging his hands on the floor like paintbrush tips for a moment with his knees still locked while the fridge cooled the top of his buttcrack.

Laurie readied the table for them to eat, placing the packets of plastic cutlery that Las Flores had thrown in the bag on the table by each of their meals. "Ooo, which one is mine?" Luke asked after unbending to a stand and slamming the refrigerator door shut.

"The enchiladas" Laurie responded flatly.

"Which ones are those?"

"The meal that isn't the tacos. Those are mine." Laurie sat in the chair in front of the tacos and extended a hand to present Luke's food to him. He seemed to need this cue. He was somehow stuck at each obvious event in the sequence of sitting and eating, like a dementia patient in a nursing home who needed to be guided through each meal. Luke's eyes lit up and he dragged the other chair out from the table and plopped down on it. Laurie picked up her plastic fork and then changed her mind, placing it back down beside her aluminum carryout container. She delicately picked up a taco and took a petite bite. She was about to take another date-appropriate bite when she looked up to see Luke digging into his aluminum container with his right hand. He scooped out half an enchilada and shoved it into his mouth. He chewed with wet and squishy noises while pawing at his food, trying to form a racketball-sized clump of beans and rice to shovel in his mouth as soon as he had swallowed the enchilada. Laurie lost her excitement over the tacos, but continued to eat anyway. She wished she were at home by herself and could enjoy her food without watching Luke's animalistic display. He reminded her of an angry toddler masticating chicken nuggets while bits and pieces fell to the ground. Luke finished his enchiladas in three and a half minutes and then leaned back in his chair. He audibly exhaled, as if he had just victoriously finished a race. Despite Laurie's hunger, she didn't want to eat her remaining two tacos so she neatly fastened the cardboard lid to its aluminum tray bottom. She stood up and walked her leftovers to the refrigerator, but she changed her mind before touching the handle. Instead, she retrieved one of the paper bags from her canvas tote in the living room and then stored her tacos in there.

Laurie's and Luke's eyes met from across the table.

Luke pressed his palms into the table top, supporting his rise from his chair. Laurie watched him stumble over to a column of kitchen drawers and his hand flopped around knocking over a bottle of multivitamins, some antacids, and saline nasal spray until he grasped the item he desired: a prescription pill bottle. He pushed down on the cap, twisted, and slid out one Xanax. When he closed the bottle, the Xanax escaped from his fingers and made the tiniest putt on the floor, a sound which did not register to him.

"It's under the cabinet closest to the fridge." Laurie told him, loudly, as if guiding the elderly.

"Thamks." He said, his jaw too relaxed to pronounce "Thanks."

He bent at the waist and hung there until he spotted the pill. Laurie thought he might fall over like a chopped tree, his butt like the treetop and his arms and legs hanging together like the trunk. He didn't though; he slowly lifted his torso back to a standing position and then leaned on the kitchen table. Laurie could hear his slow breath. He popped the pill into his mouth, but instead of swallowing it, he rolled it around with his tongue, between his gums and cheeks, like a child might do with a hard peppermint candy. He grimaced three or four times, whenever the bitterness collected on his tongue. Eventually the pill dissolved.

Luke noticed the restriction of his pants. He unbuckled his belt and undid the top button, but he didn't have the patience to bring his zipper down. Instead, he pried his thumbs between his hipbones and the jeans' waistline and brought the pants down to his ankles. He was still wearing his navy blue boxers patterned with tiny embroidered lobsters. Laurie thought for a second time that he was going to fall, but instead he stomped his feet rhythmically, freeing his feet from the pants and leaving them in the middle of the kitchen, one leg bunched up like a stored accordion and the other strewn out like it was reaching for help before it passed out from the odor of whiskey sweat.

With uneven steps, he made it to the right side of the couch and that's where he fell, the left side of his face pushing into the leftmost cushion. He was already starting to drool, adding the latest contribution to the patchwork of sofa stains. The brown and grey rings of old saliva overlapped each other's circles, like a snapshot of a fireworks show finale. She watched him for a minute. He nestled his shoulder into the cushion and followed through with his back, arriving face up, spine sinking into the couch. The snoring began with a whistling sound at first. His nasal passages were completely blocked.   "Luke." She whispered. No response. "Luke." She said with conversational volume. No response. "Luke!" She yelled. Still nothing. She picked up his right arm buy the cuff of his sleeve. His hand angled down, limp, like a dead goldfish's fins. She let his arm fall and his hand crashed into the floor. "That'll leave a bruise." She thought.

Laurie went to the refrigerator and opened the door using a dish towel. She studied the contents: half a jar of natural peanut butter, greasy nutty smears all over the outside and the lid, a bottle of soy sauce on the door, an old loaf of bread. Who keeps bread in the refrigerator? There. Her eyes rested on a package of raw chicken tenderloins in a plastic grocery bag. She grabbed the bag and pulled out the styrofoam tray of meat. The plastic outer-wrap was leaking a translucent pink liquid into the grocery bag. She closed the refrigerator door and looked back at Luke as he let out an alarmingly loud snore. She clutched the chicken and watched him as his snoring got more and more arhythmic. He would stop breathing for a few seconds at time, and then when he was about to suffocate, his lungs would go into overdrive and suck in air, overpowering his floppy throat muscles resulting in a choppy pattern of quick snoring sounds. She looked down at the chicken and pressed the tip of her index finger down into the chicken's plastic casing. When her fingernail pierced the plastic at the bottom of the finger-shaped tunnel that she had stretched into it, she tore the package open. The smoothest-looking of the seven chicken tenderloins was the one in the middle. She picked up the sleek, fascia-less chicken flesh and jiggled it. Perfect. She approached Luke, his mouth still open like the mouth of a plastic souvenir singing bass fish. Laurie dangled the pointed end of the tenderloin over Luke's tongue and made contact at the midpoint between the two gaps where his lower wisdom teeth would have been, had they not been removed a decade ago. Right after a large exhalation, the tip of the tenderloin led the way toward Luke's uvula and pushed through into his throat, much like the naturally boneless body of a slug effortlessly squeezing through a hole half its size. When the raw tender wouldn't glide anymore, Laurie pushed her meat weapon two more inches in. The snoring stopped and the sounds of the house became audible again. The humming refrigerator and the forced air through the ducts always comforted Laurie. She retreated to the kitchen table and watched silent Luke from there. The frantic contraction of Luke's diaphragm only pulled the poultry in farther. Thirty seconds had gone by. Luke was flailing hard. His eyes were open, but his muscles were too relaxed and his neural connections too slowed to reach his fingers into the back of his mouth and remove the obstruction. He looked at Laurie. She tilted her head slightly to the side. She didn't want to wave to him. He tried to establish eye contact, but she focused just behind him, like she couldn't see him at all. Forty-five seconds had gone by since the lean protein had begun to block Luke's trachea. He fell off of the couch and onto the pine floor. He was still struggling. His fingers grabbed at the edge of the coffee table but he couldn't gather the coordination to pull himself up. Laurie stepped onto the back porch to get a breath of fresh air, something Luke would never do again. She looked up at the stars and let her mind dance around while her eyes made new constellations. Laurie wondered why nobody had published their versions of the pictures the stars made. "Surely there were much better versions of star-pictures than the big and little dippers and that Orion dude and the bear" she thought. Laurie stayed outside for six minutes. She hadn't heard anything from Luke, so it was time to go back inside.

There he was on the floor, limp. She sat on the couch and noticed the tv's remote control on the coffee table. She put on an episode of *Modern Family* to keep her company. She thought about cooking the rest of the chicken, but there wasn't a clean and suitable pan in the house.

Laurie turned off Harford Road and started down the winding gravel path in her green Honda Civic. She was looking for 837 Lake Montebello Trail. She just barely spotted the rickety wooden sign hanging from the mailbox on the right with the dirty letters, 837. She was careful to slow down enough not to noisily fling gravel or make any noticeable ruts when she turned into the driveway. The driveway must have been a quarter mile long. Laurie thought, "How do people who live in lakehouses with long driveways put their trashcans and recycling bins out for collection?" Laurie had seen neighbors of hers block in the street getting their mail on the way home in order to avoid the twenty foot walk to the mailbox. Here these people were having to tote their giant garbage receptacles practically through the woods on the muddy gravel every time trash day rolled around. What if it was raining? Do you just hang onto your smelly garbage and wait until the next trash day rolls around? "That's what I would do." She told herself.

Luke was going to be tough to lift. Laurie might need a little help. Laurie exited her car, being extra careful not to make unnecessary noise. She had the code for this place in her notebook, so she looked it up typed the numbers into the keypad. "8837." It was amazing to her how many people chose variations of a home's address to hold the key to the house during the home-showing period. "Oh good, they're still there," Laurie said to herself as she spotted the rack of oars and paddles in the mudroom." She grabbed a canoe paddle and clutched it with her fist, holding it upright like a walking staff. It was almost as tall as she was. This would work. Laurie returned to her car and opened the trunk with her physical car key, rather than using the remote, which would make the car announce the trunk's opening with a loud and superfluous beep. "Alright paddle, this will be the most exercise you've ever gotten in your entire life," she told the implement, which had obviously never seen water, its finish still completely intact and its pressed wooden layers still bright and devoid of dings or scratches. Clearly this was a decoration and not an actual piece of sporting equipment.

Laurie use the paddle as a lever to hoist Luke's body out of her car trunk just enough so she could wrap her arms around him. She dropped the paddle to the gravel driveway and pulled him onto the it, placing Luke's shoulders on either side of the paddle's wide blade. She pulled his feet up toward her and grabbed the handle of the paddle with her left hand a couple inches below his knees, right below the thickest part of his calf muscles. She turned her body to set herself up for a paddle-assisted dragging, switching her grip with her left hand and wrapping her right arm around his ankles. It's a good thing the owner of this lake house hadn't bothered to take the Allington Liberty Group's advice and apply a fresh coat of wood stain to the porch in the front of the house or the deck and steps out back behind it. If they had, Laurie would be scratching up a new coat of stain and leaving obvious damage. Instead, the faint impressions from the paddle weren't noticeable at all. Laurie dragged Luke slowly up the two porch stairs, through the main entrance of the house, past the kitchen and living rooms on either side, and finally to the sliding glass door accessing the deck. She took a short break about every ten steps to catch her breath. Clunk, clunk, clunk went Luke's tarp-wrapped shoulders and head down each of the of the nine stairs. The couple then started down the short wooded path toward the lake. They stopped to rest for a minute after making it over a particularly large tree root and then continued. Laurie imagined it was just like any other time that they had headed toward the water together, but this time she felt slightly more peaceful. When they arrived at the edge of the lake, she set Luke down and unwrapped him from the tarp. His body fell on to the ground like gloopy piles of rice and beans falling from a burrito whilst some sicko removed its tortilla. When Luke's face slid down in the mud and his mouth filled with soil and lake water, Laurie imagined how the waterfront dirt must have tasted, like iron, earthworms, and money. Laurie picked up Luke's feet, holding one by the sides of her hips, much like hoisting a wheelbarrow and pushed him into the lake. She kicked at his feet and then continued prodding him with a long stick until the lake began to carry him toward the center to swallow. Laurie watched for a few minutes, enjoying the night air on her arms and breathing in the extra oxygen from the marshy plants.

Shit. What was that noise? A Black Crowned Night Heron swooped down from a White Oak tree and landed on Luke's face. What was it doing? The heron's claws gripped Luke's brow bones, likely perforating the skin above his eyelids. It squawked and then stooped down to insert its beak right into Luke's mouth. It pecked twice and then grabbed something, but what? Oh. "The chicken tender!" Laurie thought. Sure enough, the nocturnal bird had pinched the chicken tenderloin housed in Luke's throat and it tore off into the night woods, happy to take dinner back to her family.

Chapter Four

Be Easy to Live With

May 2013

As spring began to brighten into summer, it seemed the whole world was cleaning, trimming, and remodeling. The Alllington Liberty Group was no exception.

"Help me with this box, will you?" Shay called down to Laurie from atop the largest foldable step stool Laurie had ever seen.

"Sure," Laurie said, trotting over to take the box of old Allington Liberty logo branded water bottles from Shay's arms as she lowered it to Laurie. "What do we do with these?" Laurie asked, picking up one of the neon yellow plastic atrocities. A thin layer of greasy dust clung to the top layer of the forgotten freebies.

Shay explained while handing boxes of old binders and spiral-bound reference materials down to Laurie, "We stopping printing so much swag about five years ago when most of our clientele started voicing their eco friendly identities, you know, right before they would drive home to their plastic mini mansions in their giant SUVs. I guess just toss 'em."

Laurie looked down at the wattle bottles and sighed, holding onto the box. "Do you want to take them?" Shay asked, annoyed with having to pause from her clearing the top of the large bookcase. Laurie took a second to think. Shay rhythmically dropped directly to the floor the last of the boxes containing personalized business cards and stationary from former Allington Liberty Group agents who had retired or gone on to do other things. Laurie usually kept a stash of old business cards in her car for when she listed a property for a client and wanted to make it seem more popular and desirable than it was. It was proper etiquette to leave a business card on the counter when showing a property as a courtesy to the seller and the listing agent so they could have some verification of others' attendance, so a home with rows or piles of agents' cards made it look hot with lots of potential buyers. When Laurie listed a property, particularly a vacant one or a nasty turd of a home, she would scatter a few of these fake cards next to the informational packet she would display so that visitors would never think they were the only ones interested. People wanted to buy homes that other people wanted to buy. They wanted what others wanted. They wanted to win and leave the other potential buyers with what they thought of as a second-tier house, even if the homes were practically indistinguishable.

"I pass by the recycling center on my way home. I can drop these bottles there." Laurie told Shay, looking up at her, as if asking for permission to reroute the bottles from the landfill.

"Suit yourself." Shay mumbled, climbing down from the step ladder. "Allison said we needed to clean out our files and shelves too, since the whole office is getting painted and all of the furniture is getting moved." She added. Laurie nodded and headed over to her file drawer. She started pulling her possessions out and making three piles: trash, take home, and try to pawn off on somebody else.

"Shay, would you like your copy of this magazine back?"

Laurie asked, showing Shay the cover of the Spring 2010 issue of *Triumph*, a women's magazine.

"Well you might still need it. I swear by that article and I don't think I'd be with Travis if not for the advice in there. Those are the rules nobody tells you. It's been two years and I'm really happy in our relationship. It's only a matter of time before he puts a ring on it." Shay said, sticking her tongue out and displaying the back of her left hand toward Laurie, as if Laurie needed a visual of what a hand looks like without an engagement ring.

Laurie flipped open the magazine to the article upon which Shay had built her dating philosophy and instead that Laurie do the same. The article was the center spread: "Seven Secrets for Capturing the Heart of Mr. Right." The corners of the pages were now crinkled and there were two circular stains from coffee mugs, like ghosts of lattes past. The pink sticky note that Shay had left originally for Laurie was still there, wedged between two pages. It read, "This is magic. FOLLOW THIS! Love, Shay"

Laurie looked over the article for what must have been the fiftieth time.

When she had first read it about three years ago it had seemed much more sophisticated than it looked to her now. She had recently read that magazines were written at approximately a sixth grade reading level, but today the article read as even more condescending, like perhaps the intended audience was a group of small dogs.

Seven Secrets for Capturing the Heart of Mr Right

Hey girl,

Are you tired of your man not responding to your texts right away? It's because you told him you're not important. Not literally, of course, but through the ways you communicate verbally and nonverbally and through your actions and expectations for him. It's time to stop accidentally pushing him away by trying to reel him in and start deliberately attracting him to you. Before you know it, he'll be jumping into your arms and begging you to sink your hooks in.

Here's a set of seven rules you absolutely need to follow to make him want to commit to you without your having to ask him. If you follow these rules, he'll be doing everything you've been wanting him to do. You'll never have to prod him into accepting your desired relationship status. You'll never have to tell him what's on your mind because he'll be reading it. If you follow these rules, you can be sure he'll be thinking about you all the time!

1 — Be a creature unlike any other

This means it's time for the ultimate YOU. Get your hair done at the fancy salon instead of your usual. Spring for the manicure. Learn greetings and phrases in the language you've always wanted to learn and invest in your hobbies. If you start acting like the interesting person that you are, he will WANT to spend all of his time with you. Men want a fascinating girl they can show off to their friends. There's nothing sexier than a girl who can stand on her own two feet, and doesn't need a man to sweep her off of them in order for her story to be told.

Ultimately, if he doesn't flaunt you and your uniqueness, it's time for the relationship to end.

Don't talk to a man first

2

It'll take some self-control, but don't approach the hottie at the bar. Let him come to you. He has to think that you are an unattainable treasure. He must think that the only way to be with you is to win you over. You don't want to seem like some desperate reject trying to bone him.

DON'T talk to him unless he talks to you first.

3 — Be mysterious

Hide your personal items, tangible and intangible. He doesn't want to see that you have pesky family members or that you menstruate. If you have to go to the bathroom, he doesn't need to know that. Tell him, "Excuse me. I'll be right back." He doesn't want to see your hairbrush or tampons cluttering his dresser or bathroom, even if you live together. This is literal as well as figurative. Don't leave your emotional baggage all over the place for him to trip over. This means that you shouldn't tell him the details of your fight with your bestie. You shouldn't tell him when you're angry about conflict that's happening in your life. He doesn't want the drama.

4 Be easy to live with

You should avoid living with a man until it is absolutely unavoidable. When the time comes, however, answer the following question before finding yourself in an argument: "Does this really matter in the grand scheme of things?" If yes, express your needs succinctly and without emotion. Men like a woman who is easy-going.

Though men can't quite put their finger on what makes them feel comforted, be it decorative throw pillows, the scent of baking apple pie, or general tidiness, they can feel it. Make the living environment nice and cozy and he'll associate those good feelings with you.

5 Only love those who love you

If he doesn't buy you a romantic gift on your birthday, end the relationship. Let him fill your lingerie drawer! If he doesn't get you something thoughtful, like a sexy nightie, some flavored lube, or the latest piece of cookware you've been eyeing, it's time to move on!

If he stops calling you as often as he once was, note this. Maybe your daily text drops to an every-other-day greeting or picture exchange. He's just not as interested as he once was. Leave immediately. It was time to get out yesterday. He's not up for putting in the work of the relationship, so you're not interested. You shouldn't waste your feelings on him.

6 Be the life of the party

You should always have three good jokes on hand just in case you need them. While you shouldn't take over the conversation going on at the table, you should become a facilitator. Men like a woman who makes things fun and easy. Be a good listener, but be ready to make a quick transition to a different topic if you sense he's getting bored.

7 End the conversation first

He calls you. You flirt. You find a reason to hang up. End of story. You have to be the one to end your dates and conversations in order to leave him wanting more. No exceptions.

These rules may seem harsh, but we promise they'll bring you exactly what you deserve. We've found that it's not a good idea to discuss these rules with folks who won't understand them, so it can be counterproductive to talk about them with your parents or with a therapist, and it's certainly a bad idea to reference them in front of your newly scored man. Trust us. He'll be falling in love with you but you'll be the only one who knows exactly how you managed to make it happen.

"If you don't want to keep it, why don't you just pass it on to the next person who needs it." Shay told Laurie while piling boxes of garbage beside the office's small trash can. Every time Shay bent over, Laurie could see her magenta thong peeking out from the top of her black workout pants.

"Sure thing," Laurie told her. She crammed the magazine in

her box of items to take home.

Laurie didn't want to think too much about the article at work, but when she got home, she fished it out of the box and carefully placed it on the couch, as if she was situating a guest in her home. She went to the kitchen and poured herself a glass of Zinfandel, which she would only drink in front of a guest who could never speak of the experience to others. She only offered human guests red wines that she thought of as classy, worldly, and academic, as she wanted to be seen as a woman of those descriptors.

The zinfandel took Laurie's mind down a windy path of work-related thoughts. She stood in her kitchen, rehearsing tours of potentially her largest transactions.

"Welcome home!" she would say confidently. She practiced sounding bold without sounding cheesy, a feat she had not yet mastered in her rehearsals. As she sipped, she imagined how unsuccessful experiences with clients could have gone better. There were always things she wished she had done differently, as surely she was responsible in some way for a client's decision not to purchase a home. Laurie often found herself purchasing new outfits after events at work, thinking that if she had just worn a different blouse or bothered to put on a dress instead of rushing to a showing in leggings then maybe she would have made a sale. Her mind burrowed more deeply. Maybe if she looked different, slimmer, than she would sell more homes. Laurie's inebriated mind played back memories from her youth.

"You've got to do something about that child," said Aunt Linda, indicating Laurie. "She's getting really quite large and she'll never make her way socially if she doesn't learn to control herself." Laurie, age nine at the time, was unsure if she was supposed to pretend not to hear Aunt Linda's petitions to Laurie's mother or if she was supposed to chime in with an apologetic response.

"I'm so sorry that I have over-existed," Laurie retorted in her head. "I can't quite get smaller, even though I have tried and I frequently cry about it. I extend my sincerest apologies."

Laurie's discomfort manifested physically in her tensing all of her muscles in her seat and gripping her hands together, but emotionally, this moment would become one bead on a very long string of memorial beads concerning her weight. Laurie waited patiently for somebody to change the subject. Perhaps if she barely moved or shuffled, the wave of embarrassment and claims of inadequacy would wash over her and it would be over soon.

"Cheesecake? It's to die for. Price Club's bakery really makes the best desserts. Everybody should have a slice for Cara's birthday. Cara, you make us all so proud." Aunt Linda said, cutting into the glossy pie with a plastic cake server. "Mmmm, I'll just cut everybody a slice and you can grab the one you want." Small paper plates were passed around and Laurie accepted the sugary pile of graham cracker crust and mass-produced white goop that was given to her. At least it would be mildly comforting after Laurie had watched her mother patiently listen and silently agree with Aunt Linda's unsolicited critique of Laurie's body and will-power. "Laurie, you don't have to eat yours. You can leave it." Aunt Linda gave Laurie a directive look, which might have been captioned, "Don't you dare put any of that cheesecake in your mouth, you stupid, stupid girl."

Laurie had always been well aware that she was carrying extra weight. She had first begun to communicate her awareness of it when she was in first grade. Her teacher, Mrs. Grey, had assigned a worksheet that corresponded to a book they had read aloud. The family of muskrats in the book taught the children about secrets, sharing, and trust, with possible undertones of, "Tell a counselor at school if there's a creepy adult molesting you at home even though that creepy adult tells you to keep it a secret."

Laurie didn't really remember the book, but she remembered writing down "I am fat" in response to the final request of the worksheet, which read, "Write down an example of a secret that you can tell your teacher." The next day, after Mrs. Grey had engaged the students in independent work, she called Laurie to her desk.

"Laurie. It made me really sad to read your worksheet. I love you and I don't want you to think bad things about yourself. You are not fat. You are a beautiful, smart, hard-working child. I don't want to see you writing bad things about yourself. Are you okay?" Laurie nodded and held back tears. It made her happy to be reminded that her teacher loved her, but she was much more confused now. Being fat must be very bad. She had not considered this possibility. She had thought it was more of a physical descriptor than a judgment of character. From what Mrs. Grey had told her, it must be horrible to be fat. Laurie hadn't remembered any of the other parts of the Language Arts lesson, not even the morals from the molesting muskrats, but she sure remembered this.

Logically, that's how six year old Laurie knew that deep down, she must be a bad person. "It would be okay though," she told herself, "Nobody would have to know. It was a secret." Laurie's feelings about her body were re-explored daily. There wasn't any distance in her relationship with her fat cells, and sometimes she worried that this mental over-exertion was depriving other aspects of herself of regular evaluation. "If I were only thinner," she thought, "I would be so much better as a human being because I wouldn't be thinking about my weight constantly."

Laurie's mind played back one of her first social memories at the Allington Liberty Group, her first summer employed there in 2009. "It's not about selling a house." Shay said. "It's about selling an image. You don't sell brick and vinyl and lumber and drywall. You sell happiness and accomplishment. You sell stability and status. You sell community and belonging."

Laurie looked up and told Shay, "You should run the ad campaigns for all the the perfume and cologne commercials at Christmas time. I never know what those are about; it's like, people are floating up mountains and having sex with thunderclouds and I don't even know who gives cologne or perfume as a gift anyway. I mean, isn't that like giving somebody deodorant or soap? Just more expensive? Or are they not meant to be a gift? Are they just thinking that Christmas is a time when people are feeling extra desperate and they want to loved so badly that they buy expensive scents to cover up their inferior pheromones? Is that why you see so many commercials during Christmas for engagement rings?"

"What crawled up your ass today?" responded Shay.

"Nothing. Wanna go grab a coffee?"

"Yeah. Let's go."

The two young real estate professionals drank coffee and talked about their lives, pleasantly passing a slow June morning. Laurie felt the sense of support she didn't know she craved.

This had been the beginning of Laurie's friendship with Shay, she remembered as she looked back at the dog-eared magazine that housed the dating article sitting on her counter. Shay had everything together. Her life was everything that Laurie wanted. She was attractive, confident, smart, and she was focused enough to go after what she wanted. If Shay swore by this dating article, it must be worthwhile even if it was cheesy on the surface.

Laurie took a deep breath. She looked around at the nondescript walls of her townhome. She had never bothered to paint because she had never pictured this home as her destination. She took another deep breath. Laurie would turn her life around. She would lose weight. She would sell all of the houses. She would acquire an enormously impressive home for herself. She would stop murdering the men she was dating.

Laurie carried herself to bed in a cloud of determination. Tomorrow, she would start her new life.

The end of Spring was approaching. Two to three days after the beginning of students' summer vacation always marked an influx of the worst type of clients: teachers. They would make appointments to view homes as soon as they finished their last contract hours at school and they would excitedly greet their realtors, their left shoulders leading them and beginning to recover from being weighted down by heavy canvas bags full of teacher shit. They would take a million summer tour appointments to settle on the cheapest thing they could find and then a third of the time have to back out due to lack of financing.

"Make yourself at home" read the doormat of 3565 Epiphany Circle, a townhouse that had gone on the market yesterday.

"Don't mind if I do." Laurie said to herself in response to the doormat, a known trademark of the listing agent, Deborah, a kind yet forgetful woman who must have been in her early 70s. Inside, the air smelled like artificially scented pine plug-in. Gross. It was better in the finished basement, which was neutral and odor free. Laurie had shown the place to an indecisive teacher earlier that day, so she knew that it would be empty. The owner lived across town and had decided to sell the place after the last tenant had moved out. Laurie liked homes best when they were empty, free of all furnishings and stale ideas. Empty spaces meant potential. Empty spaces meant anything could happen.

Laurie's educator client had asked five questions about the townhome, which was more than any other home she had asked Laurie to show her, so maybe Jenny was getting close to putting in an offer. Laurie got voicemail after voicemail from Jenny

Hinkle, which all had the same rhythm, tone, and cadence. Jenny Hinkle clearly rehearsed phone calls before making them. The way her voice tilted up at the end of each statement making it sound like a question made her voice messages a melody of insecurity and people-pleasing.

"Hi. This is Jenny Hinkle and I'm just calling because I saw that a townhome on Cranston Square just became available and I'm interested. Please give me a call back. Thanks! Bye!"

Maybe Laurie took pity on Jenny and kept patiently showing her home after home despite very few signs of receiving any commission any time soon because Jenny was a teacher and Laurie had almost gone down that path. Laurie remembered completing education practicum, during which she had to visit, observe, and assist in eight types of public schools, one of the many requirements to earning a teaching license.

The day that Laurie had decided that teaching wasn't for her was a day of secondary practicum visiting Lake Point High School, a public school in the wealthiest neighborhood in the county.

"Oh my god, she's such a fucking bitch." said a curly-haired brunette student wearing a flannel shirt and black leggings.

"I know. I want to kill her. I can't believe she fucking made us put our essays through the turn-it-in site. Like she thinks we're going to fucking plagiarize?" a student with braces and a blonde ponytail responded. "She should know to trust us." The braces made her 's' sounds thicker, like she had a mouthful of pudding.

"We should put contact solution in her coffee. Becca said it makes you shit your brains out."

"I can't wait to see the look on her face."

Laurie wasn't sure how to bring up the conversation to the teacher whose class she was observing. It wasn't easy to approach Ms. Vance and say, "Hi, um, thanks for letting me observe your class- I just want to mention that I kind of overheard that blonde girl with the ponytail and the girl in the flannel shirt saying that they wanted to put contact solution in your coffee?" but Laurie did the best she could.

Ms. Vance did not have a flicker of reaction in her face. "Did they write down that they were going to do it?"

"Well, no, I don't think so," said Laurie, "But they said it pretty clearly."

"If there isn't any proof, there's nothing to go forward with."

"But they sounded, well, vicious," insisted Laurie.

"Yeah. They probably wouldn't do it. It's not like I would ever leave my drink around any of these kids anyway. They have way too much money and way too much access to rufies."

"Rufies? Like, seriously?" Laurie asked.

"Yeah. Seriously."

Ms. Vance had a corpse-like pallor to her face. She was so tired that she needed to prop herself up by leaning on the desk, hands clutched in fists. Laurie liked talking with people, presumably students, and she liked learning things, but the inconveniences of focused and irrational rage toward her, dodging flunitrazepam, and being overworked to make thousands of dollars less than her earning potential really deterred her from the profession.

Laurie showed Jenny Hinkle the townhome, but she never let herself get her hopes up that a teacher would make an offer. She had been disappointed too many times. At least Jenny was efficient, for which Laurie was grateful. The two of them were in and out of 3565 Epiphany Circle in fifteen minutes, which left Laurie plenty of time to get to her next appointment. This one wasn't for a client, however, it was for herself. Laurie was going to get the best deal on a home in the history of Maryland real estate. All she had to do was piece together the best contractors with the best prices in order to get the necessary work done. Laurie was determined to buy "The Shit Hole."

Laurie had been sitting cross-legged on the dirty puce-colored tiles in the kitchen when a white van from Talley Home Repair and Restoration pulled up to the house. Laurie heard the car door open and shut and she leapt up from her seated position in the middle of the floor. She had been doing something she loved doing: nothing. She had started her visit by sitting cross-legged on the matted down carpet, staring past the bloated plaster of the walls and letting her brain defragment, but then she started to get the feeling that there could be tiny critters in the flooring under her, like mites or very determined bedbugs. She continued the process of zoning out after relocating to the kitchen, where she felt the hard surfaces provided less risk of infection or infestation. Laurie felt much better if she had a few minutes each day to stare at nothing and decompress, and waiting for contractors to arrive usually gave her ample opportunity to do just that.

Laurie opened the door for Frank, the representative from Talley Home Repair and Restoration. "Hi. I'm Laurie. Come on in." She said with a an upbeat energy that she used for most of her transactions. "I know that this house has some structural damage and I'm looking for an estimate of how much it would take to restore it to a healthy condition."

"Right. Uh course." Frank said, looking around as if he expected another person to show up from down the hall and guide him around the house and its grounds.

"May I come with you while you take a look?" Laurie asked.

"I'm about to buy this house and I'm budgeting for renovating, well, everything." She told him, emphasizing the word *I'm* each time, reinforcing for Frank that she was handling this project. She was in control. She called the shots and paid the bills.

Frank gave one affirming nod before the two of them set off to inspect the inside and outside of the home's perimeter. Laurie tried hard to think of questions she could ask that would prompt Frank to teach her about the foundation restoration process. "So, um, on the average complete home renovation project, what kind of timeline is normal for foundation work?" Laurie asked.

"It depends." Said Frank without looking up. He took a foldable knife-like tool out of his pocket and dug it in to several components of the home including the baseboards, the trim around the fireplace, the plaster in half of the rooms, and a few different points of the cement between bricks outside. Whenever he found a material or surface that seemed softer than desirable he made a low "Hrrm" sound. She wondered if he knew whether or not he was doing this. Frank didn't offer many words despite Laurie's prompting questions. Frank announced, "Well, uh, I'll work up uh est-uh-mitt.

The next morning, Laurie walked into the Allington Liberty Group's office whilst checking her phone for Frank's estimate. She had checked two and half minutes earlier when she had exited her car, and then again 93 seconds prior to this while she was opening the door to the stairwell. There was still no word from Frank.

When Laurie looked up, she saw Chris, a pile of shivering sadness on the couch. He jumped up when he heard the sound of Laurie opening the office door. Laurie watched him, facing away from her and walking toward the window, as if he had some important meeting with the vinyl slats of the blinds.

"Hey," she started.

"Hi Laurie," he responded, unable to subdue the rockiness of his voice into the pool of calmness he was desperately trying to emulate. Laurie set her things on her usual desk and contemplated whether it was better to leave Chris alone or dig a little at the chance of making him feel better.

"Chris?"

"Mhmm" Chris answered, still facing away with his arms crossed in front of him.

"You seem upset. Do you want to talk?"

"No. Thanks. I'm fine."

Laurie walked into the office's kitchenette and started gathering a cup of coffee. She was thrilled to see leftover room temperature coffee in the machine's carafe as well as the almost full pint of heavy cream she had purchased last week still in the fridge. There was even ice in the freezer. The trifecta of delicious focus was at her thirsty fingertips. She made her creamy iced coffee and went to her desk.

"I'm fine, but I'll tell you since you're going to find out anyway that it's over. My relationship. My marriage" Laurie heard Chris say through the congestion of his inflamed face. He must have been talking to her despite not looking in her direction. There wasn't anybody else in the office and he wasn't on his phone. Laurie turned to look at Chris. He must have been crying for hours. His skin was blotchy and his eyes, nose, and mouth were irritated.

"Thanks for letting me know. I'm really sorry you're going through this. I'm sure it must be really hard. Just, please, if you need anything-"

"Naw. I'm good. I'm going to have a fucking party. I've already picked the date. It's September 7th. That's a Saturday. Be there."

"But don't you have to be separated for a least a year in order for the court to grant a divorce?"

"No." Chris shifted on the couch and the fabric of his khakis made a swooshy sound. "Well, I don't fucking know. Just come to the party Laurie." He looked up at her. The left side of his top lip twitched as he forced his feelings down into the pit of his stomach.

"Okay" said Laurie. She paused. "Are you up for a contract type of conversation or should we talk at a better time?"

"I'm good. Let's talk" Chris said, sitting up.

"I've got a buyer for The Shit Hole. Closing would be in early September. I can get you the offer in the next hour. Do you think you could get it ratified by the end of tonight?" Laurie asked, her face bursting with excitement despite the solemn air in the room.

"What? No way. What fucker is dumb enough to buy that turd?" Chris asked Laurie, incredulously.

"Me. I'm buying that turd and I'm going to compress that shit into a diamond."

"No way, Laurie."

"Yes. I'm doing it. Can we schedule closing for Monday, the second of September?" Chris and Laurie both examined the calendar applications on their phones.

"The second is Labor Day, so how about the next Monday, the ninth?" Chris asked.

"Yes. Absolutely. It's in my calendar. Thanks so much, Chris. I'm so excited.

As Laurie departed the office, she could feel her phone vibrating from the outer pocket of her bag. She grabbed it and saw an unfamiliar number with the local area code and decided to answer after the second ring.

"Hello?"

"Hi there, this is Frank. Is this Ms. Laurie?"

"Yes. Good morning."

"I worked on uh est-uh-mitt for yuh and fixing up the place to get it right an ready is gonna take a few things. If yuh notice there's a lot uh stuck windows on every level uh the home an yuh also got a lot uh nail pops an yuh can see 'em though the drywall in lines linin' up an down an those are prutty good indicators that yuh got some structural repair that's gotta be done. It's gonna take uh truck comin' in to fill under and reset the slab and make sure it's not gonna settle anymore into the land there. To do that we'd have to disconnect the deck there and make sure the joists and the ledger not gonna crack or damage the home. Yuh got some cracks in the basement too that need sealin' and then once that's all done yuh have to redo a lot uh the windows if you want 'em safe an workin' and we gotta inspect the doors and uh corse we can fix the nail pops and make the drywall nice for yuh. To do the whole job it's gonna be about $22,500."

Laurie heard the number and nodded her head without making a sound. She then remembered that she would have to say words into the phone in order for Frank to understand a response. "Yes. Would you consider a payment plan?"

"Oh yuh, definituhly we could work somethin' out for yuh. What's your timeline about?"

"I'm looking to close in about four months, and would want to start the work right away after closing."

"Ulright, I'll get yuh right down in muh schedule. Have a good day Ms. Laurie."

"Thank you, you too."

100

Chapter Five

Love Only Those Who Love You

Friday, September 6, 2013: Morning

One of Laurie's favorite things about being a realtor was the flexibility of her mornings. Very few people wanted to tour a potential home before 10:00 am, so she could usually sleep in if she wanted to, or she could go to the grocery store when it first opened and avoid all of the annoyances of long check-out lines, competitive parking, and those oblivious assholes who leave their carts diagonally in the aisle while they look at the nutritional facts of their frozen waffles, which they are going to buy regardless of the ingredients and sugar content. Laurie hated asking them, "Hi- sorry, may I scoot by?" She usually avoided that type of interaction altogether by turning around and going back down the aisle in the direction from which she came and then going up the neighboring aisle in order to loop around to whichever grocery item she needed. She never encountered that brand of asshole at the grocery store's opening hour. Seven in the morning was for the focused go-getters who would never leave a shopping cart in another focused go-getter's way.

Today, however, Laurie was not going to the grocery store. She arrived at Cornerstone Wellness at 9:23 and held the door open for an elderly woman using a walker and moving very slowly. The woman, probably named Marjorie or Linda or something, gave Laurie a large smile. She looked Laurie's fat body up and down and then her smile widened. She shakily said, "You must be new here! That's so good that you're putting in the work. I bet you're going to make so much progress!" Laurie tilted her head forward and forced a smile. Laurie was not new. She had been going to this gym for almost three years. Marjorie or Linda of whatever the fuck her name was new and was clearly making her way toward the "Seniors Swim! Water Aerobics" class that had started last week as part of the gym's effort to expand its clientele.

"Thank you; I sure will." Laurie replied, hiding her irritation. Laurie walked quickly to the locker room, leaving Marjorie-Linda behind. Laurie entered the only unoccupied locker bay and set her bag down on the bench. She started to unzip her hoodie, but she lost focus due to the abrasive snipping sound coming from the woman in the adjacent locker bay, sitting on the adjacent bench. Laurie was startled and frozen, staring at the back of a honey-blonde lady with a pink cable knit sweater, form-fitting jeans, and light brown patent leather boots. Was she? No. Wait. Laurie tried to get a closer look at the lady who was emitting the offensively harsh sounds. She was. The honey-blonde lady was seated, staring into the corner of the locker room, speaking in low tones through the microphone of her earbuds, and clipping her fingernails. This was a sound that Laurie couldn't tolerate. The woman's rejected nail crescents hit the locker-room floor tiles and bounced around, like the first dried beans being poured into a glass container. Laurie hoped desperately that the woman would stop casting off her excess keratin for everybody else to collect in the thick skin of their bare feet on the way out of the locker room and into the pool. Laurie unzipped her gym bag and reached for her bathing suit, but the high-pitched chops of the clippers made her wince and she had a hard time focusing enough to lay out her items and dress for the pool. Laurie always laid out her bathing suit with its backside up so that she could grab it and step into it as easily as possible, spending the minimum amount of time unclothed.

Despite the dirty and irritating elements of her gym experience, Laurie strolled into the office feeling clean and fresh, her mind buzzingly content from the caffeine of her post-workout iced coffee, her stomach calm and empty from postponing her first meal of the day until her lunch break, which she would take right before a 3:00 pm showing of a Victorian home she wished she could buy. She set her tote bag on her desk and breathed in deeply. The remaining paint particles in the air tickled her nostrils and made her slightly light-headed as she let her eyes follow the clean lines of the bright white trim adorning the edges of the muted grey walls. Laurie's automatic reaction of surprise and disruption was beginning to fade. Four months ago, the freshly painted office was an abrupt scream in her ear and she thought of their prior beige color as being "correct," but she was now beginning to forget that they had ever been different. The change had become the dominant image of the office in her mind now. The grey walls were the new default setting.

Laurie sat at the desk and took four more deep breaths. She was about to start gathering packets of comparable sales just in case she needed them today to help her clients feel confident putting a strong offer in on the gorgeous Victorian house, but she wanted two minutes of quiet first.

"Are you getting your mailing list together? I'm so behind. Ugh." Shay exploded.

"Um, no, I-"

"You didn't hear?" asked Shay.

"Hear what?"

Shay stared at Laurie blankly.

Laurie continued, "No. I'm pretty sure I didn't hear whatever ground-breaking thing you're talking about."

"Mang Homes is developing the Ridge land." Shay told Laurie, as if explaining to an elderly person who had missed life-changing news about a nuclear bombing or an alien invasion.

"The Ridge land?"Laurie asked. She didn't know why Shay expected her to know what that was.

"The Ridge family had owned the last 1400 acres of farm land within ten miles. They were the last family farm to sell since the area was rezoned. Mang must have made them an offer they couldn't turn down."

Chris appeared next to Shay and jumped in, "With the exorbitant operational costs to farmers and completely unfair food subsidy regulations, I'm surprised they lasted-"

"The point is, Mang is going to build at least another square mile of overpriced cookie cutters, so you better put on your big girl sales panties and scoop up some easy commission." Shay continued to bubble over about how easy it was to sell new construction and how she was going to flesh out her sparse collection of Fendi purses but Laurie wasn't able to listen. The words flew over her like black crows.

"Oh fuck. Fuck fuck fuck" thought Laurie. Her face must have leaked distress.

"I thought you'd be excited. You love selling new homes. This is the best news ever. You don't have to tour the buyers around; you let their sales office do the upfront legwork and you swoop in on the negotiation like a hero."

"Yeah!" Laurie said, looking up at Shay and lifting up the corners of her mouth even though they felt heavy, her best attempt at a smile. She tried to make her face appear bright and excited, instead of panicked and a little angry. "I'm going to get a coffee; do you want me to make you one?" Laurie asked Shay. "Chris? Coffee?"

"Nah, thanks." said Chris. Laurie then realized that Shay was already holding a cup of freshly brewed coffee. Shay lifted it up, indicating that she didn't need another.

"Ah. I'll be back." Laurie went into the kitchenette, set her hands on the countertop, and tried to slow her breathing down. This was bad. Laurie had better figure what to do. She couldn't be in the office for this. Laurie returned to Shay and Chris, picked up her phone, and announced, "Ooo, it looks like I've got a new showing this afternoon. I've gotta go now if I'm going to make it on time."

"Oh, nice. Where?" asked Shay.

"I don't remember the address. I'll catch you later. Bye!" Laurie told them, hurriedly collecting her bag. As she exited, she realized that she hadn't actually made a coffee before returning to Chris and Shay. Stupid. She should have; they probably thought it was really weird that she didn't. It was too late now.

Laurie piled into her Civic, throwing her bag on the passenger seat and trying to move as quickly as possible without looking hurried or stressed. When the radio streaming from her phone began to play over the car's audio system, she slammed the dashboard's button to turn it off. She needed the silence in order to think. Fuck.

John's body was on the land that Mang was about to turn into shitty homes, and if she didn't do something about it, somebody would find him.

Laurie pulled into her parking space at her townhome and took her phone out of her bag. She opened her maps app and was careful to scroll directly on the map to the location of, rather than specifically searching for Dinosaur Park. Oh no. This is exactly what she was afraid of. Dinosaur Park backed up directly to the land that Mang Homes had just acquired. John and Laurie had walked off the park's territory and continued about a third of a mile into the woods before it had happened. Those woods belonged to Mang now. Would Mang Homes flatten the land? Would the creek run as it always has been? Many of the Mang Homes communities featured man-made ponds or very rerouted natural creeks and she wondered about their different design plans and how much it costs to reroute a creek. No. Stay focused. Laurie didn't know how much time she had.

Laurie was tired and her mind began to wander again. She thought back to the day she met John about two years ago.

John was undeniably hot. His glowing brown skin hugged his muscles softly reflecting light as he moved like a calm tiger. Laurie hadn't meant to stare at him on that Saturday morning from the leftmost line at the Heart Bank & Trust kiosk within Hughes Supermarket, her hair unbrushed, her face without makeup, and her eyes lacking the nourishment of a good night's sleep. She was wearing paint-stained khaki cargo pants of capri length and a large old orange t-shirt from Habitat for Humanity, which she had never actually volunteered for, but she had thought about it a handful of times. Most of the t-shirts still in her possession at the time were free t-shirts with various logos that she didn't really think about, many of them stained from years of sweat and occasional spaghetti sauce.

John in the line to the right of her noticed her staring and he looked into her eyes. She quickly returned her lower jaw to the rest of her skull, not having realized her mouth had been agape and she broke eye contact to focus on the shiny tile floor four feet in front of her. She was so embarrassed and she brought her eyes even lower, following the stitching on her worn-out and very dirty sneakers. Her feet looked big and clompy, she thought. She refused to look up until she had finished her banking transaction, depositing two checks: one from a mail-in rebate for shaving cream and the other from her brother's reimbursement to her from his share of their mother's birthday gift, a new laptop.

Laurie could tell without looking that John's line had moved more slowly than hers had and he was still waiting, so she took the opportunity to disappear from the banking kiosk and float into the produce wing of the market, giving her a chance to breath freely and relax from the difficulty of trying to become invisible. She had no intention of buying anything, as she had only entered the market to use the bank. Her breath was retiring to its normal rate and she discontinued her gazing into the artichokes to move out the way for a shopper coming through. He didn't come through though; he stopped and greeted her.

"Hi." It was John. Shit. Oh no. Shit.

"Uh, hello." She tried to smile but she felt goofy and out-of-place, like an unkempt cartoon hippopotamus.

She started to turn away but before she could put a foot forward John asked, "So, were you staring at me?" in accusational verification.

It was time to own her actions. It felt silly to say no when she had so obviously been shooting eye lasers at his deltoids, face, legs, and ass.

"Yes," She stated. Part of her brain sent a signal to run away but her body didn't accept it and John locked eyes with her.

"Why?" he asked. She didn't know why he looked bewildered but she continued taking responsibility for her hungry eyes enjoying him back in the bank lines.

"Um, I'm sorry. I'm tired and I didn't mean to stare. It's just that you are ridiculously attractive and I was looking at you without realizing it and-" She was thankful that he jumped in and cut her off as her words slowed. She thought her reasoning must have been obvious and he somehow wanted some sort of confession and apology from her, so she was surprised when he didn't insult her or shame her.

"Ridiculously attractive, huh?"

"Yes. Like, woah."

"Well do you want to go somewhere and hang out sometime?"

"Yes. Yes, I would like to do that."

"Well would you walk out to the car with me?"

"Um, you're not like a serial killer or anything like that, are you?"

"No."

"Okay." They left the piled-high displays of apples, pears, and carrots and exited the store. The sun was shining brightly through the dancing oak leaves, making delicate shadowy patterns hop around on the asphalt of the parking lot. She kept just a couple steps behind him, just in case. He turned at his black Nissan Altima. She stopped about four feet away and he swung around to the driver's side door to retrieve a pen. He looked back up at her and closed the door, returning to her as she kept her distance. Laurie always envisioned potential situations where she might become the victim of a kidnapping, so she never put herself in front of the car doors of people she didn't know and trust. She imagined that any moment an unmarked van would pull up next to her and a man would slide open the van door, pushing her into the stranger's car. The stranger would drive off with her, never to be seen again. The van driver and the stranger would surely cage her in a dark and damp basement. They'd slowly cut her to bits, starting by sniping her eyelids vertically with scissors. She'd never blink again and her severed eyelids would droop down over her eyeballs, bleeding and eventually oozing into her face.

"Okay. Well I'm going to give you my number and you call me when you want to see me." He scrawled his phone number on the back of his bank receipt. He also wrote in all capital letters, "JOHN."

"Okay. Thanks. Do you want my number just in-"

"No. Because you have my number and you'll call me if you want to see me."

"Okay. I will." She smiled at him, aiming for a sexy expression but falling short in her unshowered and semi spacey state. He got into his car and drove away. Laurie walked back into the store, completely forgetting that she didn't need anything. She did a lap around the aisles anyway, feeling especially empowered by the time she got to the freezer section.

Laurie paced back and forth in her apartment bedroom. Should she call John? Of course not. He had surely forgotten that he was feeling lonely for those five minutes in the grocery store a few days ago. On the other hand, what did she have to lose? The worst thing that could happen was that he would tell her that he's not actually interested. He could possibly be mean about it. Was that the worst thing? Actually, it wasn't. He could pretend that he was really interested and he could lure her out by herself and then murder her and store her body parts in a laundry basket in his basement until he got tired of not being able to use the laundry basket for either soiled or freshly laundered clothes. Maybe if he was in fact a psycho, like in this scenario, he would put both his soiled and clean clothes in the *same* basket. Gross. Laurie pictured John getting annoyed with Laurie's gooey pile of limbs and deciding to clean up his life by loading her, piece by piece, into a top-loading washing machine and washing her with hot water. It would be almost like she was slow cooking in a crock pot. When the wash cycle would finish, he would check to see how much of her had melted away, and then he'd add a little more laundry detergent, close the top again, and restart the washer. Her bones would hit the sides with a loud clanking and he'd have to turn up the television in order to drown out the racket. He'd have to shift the washer back to its original position after the couple occasions that it threw itself off balance due to the unwieldiness of her body. Laurie imagined the triglycerides melting out of her adipose tissue and majorly contributing to the fatbergs in the sewer system that she felt like she was always reading about. That would be the worst thing that could happen if she called John. Laurie would become a contributing glob of several fatbergs in the sewer system and nobody would care that she was gone, especially not John.

Laurie looked at the paper and dialed his number.

Laurie and John never fucked. She had imagined the occasion many times, particularly when she would relax and touch herself. She used the memory of his strong, warm mouth and full lips kissing her neck while his hands would massage her back, thighs, and butt. She would press herself against his hard body, wanting to feel close to him and he would feel the heat rising between her legs. Sometimes he would unbutton her jeans and slide two fingers across her vaginal opening and then pull some of her wetness out and present it to her, as if she didn't know she was an open hydrant down there, physiologically craving his hard cock. He would say into her ear, "Fuck. That purring pussy is so fucking wet." He would put the tip of his tongue on a rolling droplet of her secreted lubrication and then pop his fingers into his mouth like his was enjoying the residue of a popsicle, sucking on the stick to get the last bit sugar out of the wood fibers. The vibration from his groaning with unbridled delight would resonate in his chest and tracheal tree and tickle her breasts from the inside, as if the sound was entering through her erect nipples and dancing in her pillowy tissue.

John would usually initiate their intimacy in a semi-public place, like the backseat of his car in the parking lot of the mall after dark. This made each occasion all the more memorable for Laurie because sometimes she would still think of John when passing by places they were together. August of 2011 was filled with intense, cyclical pleasure and wanting from Saturday the sixth when they first met in that grocery store she now avoided as to not be reminded of him, all the way through Friday the twenty-sixth, which was the last time she saw him.

Their last date was a spontaneous sushi lunch followed by a walk downtown when John wound up with an unexpected half day off of work and Laurie cancelled a home showing just to see him. They entered several shops and laughed and talked as they strolled and the minutes flew by. They found themselves in the stacks of a library, Laurie's ass propped on metal shelving and pushing a line of books slightly further and further back as John's hips rocked pressing into her. They shared slow and sloppy kisses and playful bites and licks. John reached his hand in to the top of Laurie's black v-neck t-shirt and lifted her left breast out of her bra. He slurpingly kissed it, opening his mouth as much as he could without unhinging his jaw. His throat pulsed as his sucking drew her nipple so far back that she thought it brushed his uvula. When he released and brought his mouth up again to kiss her, the air chilled her exposed boob, still wet with his saliva and tender from its rigorous pumping.

"Goddamn, you're fuckin' flexible" John said as he lifted her left ankle up close to his ear with ease and surprise. Laurie's right leg was cradling his back. Laurie felt like she might explode if she didn't have him. She unbuttoned his jeans and his already hard dick became so engorged that the right and left elements of his zipper began to unengage from the building pressure.

Footsteps. Either the noise didn't register with John or he was pretending not to hear.

"John," Laurie whispered softly into the library air. The footsteps came closer. John had not stopped to replace Laurie's leg or her bare tit or his own pants' button or zipper. "John." She said more sharply. The footsteps slowed and then there was a loud thud as they watched a hardback Stephen King novel land in the aisle about ten feet from them.

"It's 4:55," said a petite librarian, "We close in five minutes." She didn't show herself or pass by to pick up the copy of *Delores Claiborne* that she had thrown to warn them of her presence.

"It's time to go" Laurie told John.

John kissed Laurie goodbye outside of the library after they exited, holding hands. "See you tomorrow?" John asked.

Laurie nodded, fully smitten. "Want to do dinner at Les Fraises tomorrow at 7:00?"

"Oui oui, ma chérie" said John, lifting Laurie's chin and planting one last enveloping kiss on her whole mouth.

On Saturday, August 27, 2011, Laurie made herself a notably delicious iced latte. She frothed the milk in a blender bottle, which gave her a coffee shop quality drink with minimal cost and effort. She relished every sip as she got dressed, putting on her black and white koala print blazer, a garment which she rarely felt confident enough to wear. Laurie often found herself avoiding loud clothes, believing that they were reserved for people who wanted to call attention to their bodies. This belief left her wearing mostly black pants and almost exclusively solid colored tops to work. Today she put her hair in a playful high ponytail and smiled as she tied a red ribbon in a bow over the boring black elastic hair tie. She winked at herself in the mirror and then left her home to lead three energetic home showings. They were all within five miles of each other, so her Saturday morning felt efficient and satisfying. She was back home by 2:00 pm and was still bouncing with happy energy. Laurie removed her small black overnight bag from her closet and packed the essentials first: her makeup pouch, her toothbrush and travel-size toothpaste, her deodorant, and her phone charger. Then she opened her bottom dresser drawer and rummaged through various seasonal items, pushing aside scarves she never wore, a two-piece bathing suit, and a gifted pair of bootsocks that hurt her calves when she tried them on. Ah. There. She felt the straps of her black, lacy lingerie dress. She wasn't quite sure what to call this garment as she had heard lingerie advertisements refer to a thing like this as a teddy, chemise, or negligee and she wasn't sure what the differences were between those garments. Without thinking about it too much, she poured her sex-dress into her overnight bag and gave it an affirmative nod. She then piled underwear, leggings, and two different shirt options on top.

Laurie parked on the street around the corner from Les Fraises at 6:56, checked her eyeliner in her car visor mirror, and briskly walked toward the restaurant, bouncing as she stepped. Her strappy summer flats accentuated her glossy toenails, which she had painted a deep wine red a half hour before leaving. She opened the cafe's door at 7:00 sharp, smiling. She was partially relieved that she didn't see John right away. She would look sexier sitting at the table with a cocktail that she would looking around for him and then meeting him where he was already seated.

"I'd like a water and a gin and tonic, please" Laurie told Rita, her server. All of the servers were dressed in crisp black and white button-down shirts with black neckties and black pants. Laurie's gratitude for never having been required to wear a necktie as part of a uniform crossed her mind. She thought about how a necktie would never sit the right way against her boobs and would seem comical, like a clown sporting freakishly large shoes or a stupidly tiny hat.

At 7:04, Rita plopped Laurie's gin and tonic onto the table, the white tablecloth dampening the noise. "Thank you" said Laurie, smiling. Laurie waited a minute before taking a sip. She stared at her drink and then let her eyes wander across her table and bounce around to the other tables. Which entree on other peoples' tables looked the best? A middle-aged man and woman were digging into two salads laiden with very rare sesame-crusted ahi tuna. They had a basket of crusty-looking bread between them. Surely there was a ramekin of fresh butter alongside the bread, Laurie thought. It would be a such a shame if this restaurant didn't use real butter. There was a table of five college-aged friends passing around bites of their different meals. They were laughing and taking turns spitting out one-liners that Laurie didn't understand. She missed having enough inside-jokes with her college buddies to fuel an entire Saturday night's dinner conversation. Two men in their early thirties were enjoying steak frites and a croque madame. Were they dating? Were they friends who weren't afraid of people assuming they were dating while out at an adorable French cafe on a Saturday evening? Laurie's eyes followed the ornate crown moulding around the room's perimeter. She looked at the baseboards. She followed the chair rail around with her eyes and admired the understated end caps at each archway and window. She imagined how this place would look with wainscoting and she was a little surprised the owners hadn't chosen bright white wainscoting for their restaurant. Maybe it would be too much white when taking into account the traditional white tablecloths?

Laurie pulled out her phone from her purse to see that it was now 7:21 and there wasn't a text or missed phone call from John. John wasn't usually late. Why hadn't he arrived yet? She didn't want to seem needy, so she would wait until 7:30 to send him a text. Of course he would arrive by 7:30 and she wouldn't have to text him, she thought.

Rita swiftly landed next to Laurie's table like a robin

gliding from branch to branch in a tall oak tree. "May I get you anything?" she chirped.

Laurie finished her gin and tonic in two gulps. "Yes please. I'd like another gin and tonic," she said, handing Rita the empty glass.

"Absolutely," Rita answered, already en route to the kitchen by the time Laurie finished saying the word tonic. Laurie checked her email on her phone. There was nothing interesting to distract her and her nervousness was growing as the seconds crawled by. It was now 7:29. She straightened her back and sat more upright in her chair, leaning forward and then backward so that she could see the sidewalk in both directions leading to the restaurant. There was no sign of John. Laurie exhaled and began to draft a text.

"Hey! I'm at Les Fraises! We said 7:00, right?" Laurie stared at her phone, waiting for a response. She hoped John was okay. What if he had gotten into a car accident? What if he was being air-lifted to a hospital right now? She checked the sidewalks again. There was no John. Laurie took a deep breath and opened Instagram. She scrolled through photos of friends she hadn't spoken with in years. Kelly Ann Hopkins just got engaged. Jaden Brown is in Italy with his girlfriend. They're drinking wine and loving each other. Scarlett Thompson just landed a role in the ensemble of the Broadway musical *Peter and the Starcatcher*, scheduled to open next year. Great. She deserves this, Laurie thought. She was so good in the musical back in high school. Laurie had almost auditioned for that production of *How to Succeed in Business Without Really Trying* but she had decided not to. She wondered if Scarlett had been in every show in high school. Laurie had only seen two of her high school's musicals and she found herself wishing she had seen all four of them. There was still no text from John. It was now 7:40. Laurie looked at John's contact page in her phone. She called him. One ring. Two rings. "Pick up, John," she huffed in her mind. Three rings.

Four. Voicemail. She hung up. At 7:45 she called him again and left a message: "Hey John, I'm here at Les Fraises and I just wanted to call and make sure you're okay. I'm looking forward to seeing you. Hope you get here soon. Bye!" Laurie always lifted her voice with positive energy to deliver the final words of a voicemail. Her "Bye!" sounded like she was in line for a roller coaster or a funnel cake at an amusement park and she had to end the message so she could enjoy a thrilling ride or something hot and delicious.

At 7:49 she called John again. This time, she heard John's voicemail recording after one and a half rings. Shit. What? What just happened? She checked her text messages again. There was still no note from John.

Tears welled up in Laurie's eyes. She watched the white tablecloth absorb the droplets falling from her face. Now she just wanted to leave. Where the fuck was Rita? Laurie lifted her head to find Rita watching her tables from the wall by the kitchen's entrance. She made eye contact through blurry. Tears. Rita swooped in to rescue Laurie who was now red-faced and tense.

Laurie stated calmly, "I'd like the ahi tuna sandwich, plated, with the fries, but I'd also like a to-go box and the check. Thank you so much." Rita nodded and went directly to the computer kiosk to input Laurie's order and print her check. Whew. Laurie still hoped John was okay, but she thought about how unlikely it would be that he was experiencing some sort of emergency. Did he stand her up because of something she said? Had he ever even liked her at all?

Two minutes later, a worker from the kitchen appeared by Laurie's table to verify her order. "So, you don't want your food to-go or do you?"

"I would like it plated but then I would also like an empty to-go box. Thank you." Laurie said, trying to smile like she normally would, but coming off like a hurt animal trying to hide its injury.

"Oh, okay. So you want the box at the same time as the food or after?"

"At the same time, please, along with the check as well, please. Thank you." Laurie was running out of conversational sanity. When the kitchen representative didn't leave her table, she continued to explain, "I have to leave unexpectedly, but I'm also hungry."

Laurie was grateful that the food arrived four minutes later. She handed her credit card to Rita and took three large bites of the sandwich, before sticking it in her to-go box and dumping the fries on top. Rita had her credit card back to her in twenty seconds and then left for the kitchen without attempting an awkward goodbye. "Thank you, Rita," Laurie thought.

On Saturday morning, November 12th of 2011, Laurie put on jeans and her favorite hoodie. It was sunny enough outside that Laurie wanted to leave her apartment and do something, but she couldn't think of an errand that needed running. She had a fully stocked refrigerator from yesterday's grocery store trip and there weren't any household items that she needed. Sometimes on days like this when she woke up with a desire to go out but she couldn't think of any friends who would want to receive an invitation to an activity at 7:00 am, she went to the local thrift store and bought a new kitchen appliance, secondhand. Laurie wandered into her kitchen and opened her cabinet where she shoved small appliances from occasions like this. There was the pasta maker, the ice cream maker, the immersion blender, the electric wok, and the sandwich press. Her cabinet was getting full of gadgets that she had learned something from, but would ultimately take back to Second Chance Thrift and Salvage in a big cardboard box that would be in the trunk of her car for at least two weeks first. Laurie didn't need another kitchen appliance, even if it was practically free. She decided to look for a new park to explore.

Laurie went to her computer and looked at the already open browser with twenty-seven tabs. She clicked around and closed nine of the tabs and then typed "Parks near me" in the address bar of the tab with a sushi menu that she need three days ago. The sushi menu's disappearance and the emergence of Google Maps satisfied her, like she was putting away part of her past week. She searched for a park. It turned out there were fifteen parks within reasonable driving distance. Which one sounded the most interesting and rejuvenating? Definitely Dinosaur Park. She looked at how to get there and committed approximate directions to memory. It was only a twenty-six minute drive.

Laurie parked in the lot and got out of her Civic. "Who designs these things?" Laurie thought. She wondered about the park's funding and who got to decide that this land should be filled with large, plastic dinosaurs spaced far apart to walk through and take pictures with, with various small playgrounds every 2000 yards or so. Sometimes she wished her income depended on creating spaces of whimsy and wonder for families instead of slinging real estate. Laurie put her phone and keys in the front pocket of her hooded sweatshirt and left everything else in the car. She headed toward the most obvious trail's entrance, breathing in the crisp autumn air and letting the whooshing sounds of the wind blowing through the trees and the static-like ruckus of the crispy leaves rubbing shoulders fill her ears. As she walked, some of the tension in her back loosened and her arms began to swing comfortably instead of staying rigidly posted at their usual stances, ready to make friendly gestures and greet potential buyers.

Almost in a nature-induced trance, Laurie came upon a clearing in woods where a neon orange stegosaurus held its head up proudly while the morning sun rays danced across its thagomizer. Laurie had learned that a "thagomizer" was a stegosaurus' set of four fierce spikes on its tail by reading the park's historic plaque. She also learned that a stegosaurus had seventeen plates, called scutes, which she had always assumed were made of bone but are actually made of osteoderms and had a lattice-like structure filled with blood vessels. The plaque also told Laurie that the stegosaurus was a social creature who traveled in a herd and that it was herbivorous. She looked around and didn't see any other dinosaurs in sight.

"Poor Stella," Laurie offered to the plastic creature, assuming her name, "Where are your friends? I bet you want to go to the salad bar with them and talk shit about that asshole triceratops." Laurie waited a minute for Stella to answer. If Stella had answered, she might have said something like, "What's a triceratops?" as a triceratops would have lived during the late cretaceous era, about 110 million years after the stegosaurus lived and the two dinosaurs would have never crossed paths, but Laurie didn't know this and none of the historical plaques in the park happened to explain the relative timing of the dinosaurs' existences. Laurie continued, "It's okay. I'll be your friend. Let's take a photo together." Laurie pulled out her phone, leaned her face toward Stella's face, and took six or seven photos. "Cute!" she said, cheering up the late jurassic critter.

The new friends parted as Laurie headed toward the park's informational board at the start of another trail. Laurie examined the color-coded map and determined that if she were to walk about a quarter-mile up the Red Trail, she would find an overlook described by the park's posted brochure as "Beautifully stunning."

When Laurie reached the top of the overlook, she wondered how much time was enough time to take in the scenic view. She had looked briefly and was about to walk away and then she remembered the wording of the brochure and thought she should stare out over the cliff for a few minutes to make sure she wasn't missing the appeal. She stared down over the cliff's rocky edge until she felt small and insignificant in a calming, satisfying way.

The sound of a trail-runner approaching from the other end of the Red Trail brought her back to her default state of being very conscious of herself. She looked up to see where the runner was so she could be sure to get out of his or her way. It was a man in red basketball shorts and a tight white t-shirt. The man came closer. Shit. The man was John. John was the trail-runner. Shit. Shit.

Laurie wondered if he would remember her or if he had completely forgotten about their three weeks of obsession, during which time they had spoken every day. Should she pretend to be invisible? Which way should she look? Shit.

Laurie stared over the edge of the cliff, hoping John would run right past her. He was clearly in excellent health and was not suffering from bed sores in a hospital whist missing his arms and legs, spending his days praying for enough brain function to return to him so that he might learn to text her back using his teeth. The rays of sunlight peeking through the trees bounced along his firm neck and highlighted the definition in his chest, illuminating his collar bone and pectorals. "Damn, he's so good-looking," Laurie thought to herself every time she stole another glance out of the corner of her eye.

John slowed down. "Why? Keep running, John," Laurie thought.

"Hey you!" John greeted Laurie from six feet away. She turned her head and met his eyes. For some reason, he had his arms outstretched for a hug. "Oh! Sorry. I guess I'm all sweaty and gross" he said, accompanying his non-joke with a laugh. Laurie followed his cue for light-hearted conversation despite her anger. Her blood was racing, yet she felt cold. Her fingers tingled and she felt like she was floating from her knees up. She used all of the strength in her face to lift the corners of her mouth up into a smile.

"How are you?" Laurie asked, tilting her head to the side 30 degrees, like a dog might do upon hearing an unidentifiable noise.

"I'm doing well! Just getting in my run. You look great!" John told her. Their next few lines of conversation were not memorable until John told Laurie, "I usually stretch at this overlook" and she imagined his perfectly proportioned body in various yoga positions. Then the poses started to happen after a few shoulder swings and John's quick adjustment of his neck and upper vertebrae, which was somehow also sexy even though it would have been borderline disgusting had another person's neck made the same cracking noises. John went into a runner's lunge, facing away from the cliff and then lifted into Warrior 1. Laurie counted him take five breaths, which he did too audibly, as if he were performing and not just respirating. His left arm lowered and stretched out toward the overlook while he repositioned his feet and other arm into Warrior 2. The loud breathing continued. John moved through his remixed version of a sun salutation until his body went into a gorgeous mountain with his asscheeks as the summit, also known as downward-facing dog. He then lifted a leg, which in yoga is called Eka Pada Adho Mukha Svanasana, but both Laurie and John knew this pose as downward-facing dog with one leg in the air. Laurie sometimes did the same stretch at home and it made her hips feel great. She thought about joining in with the peaceful movements but she kept to herself. John might have thought that Laurie would leave once he began his stretches, based on the fact that he was moving much more quickly once he began to repeat the sequence on the other side, facing the overlook. Laurie waited. As John took his second deep inhalation in after lifting his opposite leg from downward-facing dog, Laurie flew toward him, grabbed the front of his sky-high shin with both of her arms and supported his leg on her shoulder.

She half-squatted and then threw John's leg over his downward-facing head, which sent him tumbling downward over the cliff.

"Ouch," Laurie mouthed to John when his head hit a ledge and he left a bloody splotch on the dirty rock. John continued to tumble, like a rag doll who had been kicked down the stairs. Laurie glanced in both of the trail's directions to make sure nobody was coming before she continued to watch John fall. Now he was log-rolling, his arms still stretched out over his head, clearly not giving up on the flexibility training portion of his workout. He bounced over a few more rock faces and Laurie compared the sound of John's neck cracking intentionally at the beginning of his stretching to the sound of his upper vertebrae actually separating and his nose breaking and a few more of his bones snapping and shattering. The sounds were similar but Laurie couldn't decide which ones were more annoying. Finally, John's sculpted ass receded into a crevice near the bottom of the cliff, ending his tumbling act. His red basketball shorts were no longer visible. Laurie could see John's limp and broken forearm poking out when she looked as far as she could from the cliff's overhang, but a large gust of wind soon buried it with crisp, autumnal leaves.

A person walking through the talus and scree of the valley might have been able to spot John under the leaves, for a week or two, but it seemed Marylanders close to Dinosaur Park preferred to stay on the trails instead.

Friday, September 6, 2013: 11:40 Pm

Laurie's heart was still racing as she sat in the parking lot of Dinosaur Park, an empty black duffel bag in her trunk. In a private browsing tab on her phone, she had been studying the trail map for nearly nine minutes. Laurie was both amped and tired. Since hearing about Mang Homes' land development plans this morning, she had tried to fill the hours until it would be dark enough to return. She had been distracting herself with coffee and whatever news programming she could find. As long as she didn't hear anything that could be traced back to her, she would be okay. Laurie spent the majority of the afternoon following a news story about poachers having killed 41 elephants in Hwange National Park in Zimbabwe. Fucking poachers. Apparently industrial cyanide is really easy to procure in Zimbabwe because of its use in gold mining. Laurie wanted to know more about how cyanide selectively dissolves gold from ore, but she also wanted to keep her Internet search history clean at a time like this. She was avoiding Googling the words cyanide, poison, and kill. Laurie felt sad as she imagined the large and helpless elephant bodies scattered throughout the African park, like little grey mountains, their last treat having been from their own poisoned salt trays. She wondered how much money the elephants' ivory tusks were worth. How much money was enough to make a person kill an innocent elephant? Laurie pictured poachers running around Hwange Park in the middle of the night cutting off tusks and putting them in a duffel bag. Laurie thought about John's body and how she was going to fit him into her duffel bag. How much of him would be left? Would he look like a nasty raggedy corpse or would his body already have skeletonized? If the latter, Laurie might be able to pick him up easily and return to her car like a poacher with a bag of ivory tusks.

Laurie neatly folded the duffel bag and put it in a backpack, which she wore into the park. The pack only contained the duffel bag and her best flashlight. The night air was crisp and pleasant on her face and the harmonious sounds of crickets, katydids, and cicadas comforted her and hid the sounds of her footsteps against the blue trail. According to the map, if she followed the blue trail, which was basically a flat, even bypass around the western half of the hilly red trail, but then she proceeded north for about an eighth of a mile instead of following the eastern curve of the trail, she could find the base of John's death cliff about a quarter mile eastward from there.

Laurie couldn't believe that she found him so quickly. She remembered how he had tumbled and a rocky mouth had swallowed his butt. It was like he had fallen into a sedimentary bassinet. Perhaps his final day showed similarities to one of his first, cradled, helpless. John's white cotton t-shirt was gone, disintegrated along with practically all of his flesh. Laurie could only halfway believe that she actually found him, but sure enough, his red polyester nylon blend double-weave basketball shorts were still hanging from his femurs. They looked warped in places. Having witnessed John's body's autolysis, corpse bloat, and decay, those shorts had seen some shit. John's shorts must have met vultures who feasted on John's flesh and been a temporary hammock to insects galore. The shorts probably learned first-hand that maggots prefer muscle tissue to fat tissue. Laurie's was grateful for her fortunate timing. She thought about the various phases of human decomposition that would have been so much worse that this one. She didn't know if transporting John's body would be possible if she had heard about Mang's land development deal shortly after he had fallen. What if she had had to return just as his organs were beginning to liquify?

Laurie took a deep breath before embarking on John's skeletal inventory. His bones seemed to be all there at first glance. Of course the tiny ones didn't matter. Nobody would pick up the littlest inner ear bones caked in muck from the soil and identify them, saying, "Hey! Where's the rest of this skeleton?" Laurie imagined the tiniest bones, the hammer, anvil, and stirrup having been digested by a scavenger bird who had ripped John's ears off of his head and swallowed them whole. The type of bird who ate John's ears was the type of bird who would have failed the Stanford marshmallow experiment on delayed gratification by Walter Mischel. Laurie often thought about this experiment since learning about it in her college Psychology class. The results suggested that children who delayed their eating of a gifted marshmallow after having been promised a second marshmallow as long as they waited to eat the first one were found to be more successful in life as shown by SAT scores and parental descriptions. Laurie often wondered which type of kid she was. Would she have eaten the first marshmallow soon after having received it or would she wait for a second marshmallow to appear? Laurie never bought into the validity of this experiment, mostly because she knew as a child that she would have made her marshmallow decision based on her perception of the marshmallow-eating culture around her and what other people might think of her in either scenario. Laurie's mind flitted about college memories, marshmallow experiments conducted on preschoolers, and her self identity while surveying the dirty bones. She looked down and noticed that John was missing a shoe. Fuck. He was missing his whole foot. Where the fuck was his other shoe, hopefully with his foot bones inside of it? Shit.

Laurie scanned the area using her flashlight until she found the other shoe, and sure enough, it looked like all of his foot bones were still in there. The shoe was heavy, containing a goop of boney mud where more than the hundred plus muscles, tendons, and ligaments had once kept the 26 human foot bones in the perfect arrangement for walking, jumping, climbing, meeting in 33 joints. Laurie loaded John's remains into her duffel bag. She moved quickly, but with the care not to leave any parts of John behind. John's keys and phone crossed Laurie's mind, but she didn't take the time to search for them because she doubted the finding of either item would trigger a search for human remains.

As Laurie carried the duffel bag back she thought about what she might say if she were stopped. What was the believability she was toting tennis gear? Were there even tennis court around here? What about extra clothes from a photo shoot in Dinosaur Park that she had accidentally left behind but needed to retrieve before tomorrow? Was she the model or the photographer? Laurie was relieved and tired when she returned to her car. She decided to be grateful for the shoulder workout, as she had had to switch carrying arms for John's body every 200 feet or so. Honestly, she had thought John would weigh more, but at this point, he didn't quite top 30 pounds.

Chapter Six

Be the Life of the Party

Saturday, September 7, 2013

W hen Laurie woke, her eyes snapped open. Her first thought was to check on John's body, which she had hastily stashed in the storage closet under her stairs when she got home from last night's rescue mission around 1:45 am. Her second thought was coffee. She got up and went to her kitchen. Checking on John was ridiculous, right? It's not like he would have gotten up in the middle of the night to use the bathroom. Laurie made herself an iced coffee in her favorite to-go tumbler. She left it on her kitchen island while she showered and dressed herself in jeans, fall boots, and a black t-shirt with a black sweater. She would have to figure out what to do with John after her two home showings this morning, both of which had been scheduled overnight by the Allington Liberty Group's automated online scheduling system. Laurie looked at her showing appointment calendar. Both showings were for Steven and Clarissa, the wishy-washy couple who had been looking at homes with Laurie practically since the beginning of the year. At least now that it was five months later than the last time she saw them, she might figure out the answer to whether or not Clarissa is pregnant.

After a quick walk through the second townhome, Steven

and Clarissa exchanged silent eye contact and engaged in a shared nod. "We'd like to make an offer on the first home we saw today, the one on Fiddleson Peak." Laurie was stunned. Not only had she envisioned the couple farting around in real estate limbo forever, but she was fairly certain she could get them the house relatively easily. The home on Fiddleson Peak was listed under The Allington Liberty Group and she wasn't aware of any other existing offers.

"That's fantastic! Congratulations! Let's get the ball rolling!" Laurie exclaimed. "If you don't mind my asking, what made you fall in love with the Fiddleson Peak house? It seems like you were on the fence with so many other properties."

"Fall in love?" Steven asked, not quite mocking her, but questioning her choice of words.

Clarissa chimed in, "It's just time to find a place to live. We've just got to make some choices and roll with them, I guess."

"That's so excellent. Really, congratulations. Right after we go over details, I can head to my office and email you the contract for your approval before I submit it. You can e-sign it."

Laurie locked the door behind Clarissa and Steven and then drove to her office. She opened her windows and let the fall air tickle her ears. She smiled and turned up the volume on the radio, finding herself shamelessly singing along to Lorde's *Royals*.

Laurie energetically began to work on the Fiddleson Peak offer for Steven and Clarissa once she got to the Allington Liberty Group's office. The only other people in the office were Chris and Peg, so it was much easier for her to focus than when the office was buzzing with other realtors trying to build a hive full of their commissions. After a few minutes, she heard an exasperated huff.

"Oh no-" Chris said to himself, his shoulders dropping as he looked at his phone.

"What's wrong?" Laurie asked.

"I want to go prep for my party tonight but the Rooster couple wants to see 49 Barringer Road and I really don't want to miss out. They've been antsy to make an offer and I don't want them to wait and have a lot of time to reconsider."

"What do you have to do to prep?"

"I already shopped; all the booze is in the garage fridge and most everything else is in paper bags in the pantry. I need to get the fire pit started and have it burning for a couple hours before anyone gets there so it's not a mess of lighter fluid and smoky dry leaves."

"I could do that for you if you need to bag the Roosters," said Laurie.

"Could you really? I would be so grateful. This house has a fucking ridiculous $18,000 fire pit smoker combo outside and I've never used something like that. It's like if Guy Fieri's house were on MTV Cribs, this would be the centerpiece."

"That's awesome. Just text me the address and the codes and I can be there by four. I don't have anything I need to do this afternoon. I'm dying for a change of scenery anyway," she said, looking around the room, pausing at Peg, whose head was bouncing back and forth from left to right along with the sound of the copy machine."

Laurie's phone chimed.

Chris' text message read:

100 Classic Way

Olney, MD 21536

Door: 1005

Pool: 5050

Tennis Courts: 9437

"This place has tennis courts? Shit."

"Yeah."

"Where are the owners?"

"Belgium."

"Damn."

Laurie just had to pick up one thing: John's body. When she got to her house around 2:30, she picked up her mail and poured herself a glass of water, just like any day she arrived at home. This would be a lot easier than some of her other transports, as John was now light and compact, thanks to nature, the animals, and the slimy miracle of bacteria. When Laurie opened the storage closet's creaky door, she imagined that he was Harry Potter before he had ever heard of Hogwarts. "Harry, where's Ron?" she asked John's body in her best impression of London dialect. "Have you got your wand with you? Are the Dursleys still givin' you 'ell?" She responded as John's body impersonating Harry Potter, "I haven't met Ron yet and I don't 'ave a wand and Dudley Dursley locked me in 'ere and I dun died abou' it."

Laurie dragged John's body to the door between her living room and the garage and then wiped the sweat from her brow. She stopped and did a few lunges, moving into a runner's stretch on each side, relieving her legs and lower back from the small amount of tightness that last night's carrying had caused.

Laurie grabbed her keys from her purse that she had

thrown on the couch and she used the remote to pop the trunk open. "Beep!" She found the way the car's trunk-opening sound bounced off the cement floor and echoed between the garage walls very satisfying. Laurie dragged John to the back of the car and positioned herself sumo-style, legs wide apart, gripping the handles of the John-stuffed duffel with her fists. "Oh. This must be why they call this a deadlift," she said quietly. She placed John on the car's back bumper and then moved her arms one at a time to under him, his bony weight resting on the undersides of her forearms. She planted her feet more closely together, squatted slightly to get more leverage under him, and popped her arms up with enough power to lift him over the trunk's lip in. She figured that the exaggeration of her movements while carrying John would somehow count as a workout.

Laurie's GPS told her that she would be approaching her destination on the right in 100 feet, but all she could see was the autumnal leaves, branches, and tree trunks of the deciduous forest through which Classic Way was winding. Sure enough, when she slowed down and peered carefully out of the passenger's side window, she saw a humble gravel driveway with a small white sign staked into the ground. The black letters marked the address. She turned onto 100 Classic Way's entrance in her grumbling Honda and the driveway widened. The gravel turned into a grey paved surface with lots of sparkling bits. It was like the asphalt was loaded with chunks of quartz. How far off the road was the house? She has already driven a quarter of a mile. When she squinted, she could see that the enormous mansion was ahead. As she kept driving, more structures came into focus. There was a pool house and a guest house. She wondered where she should park. There was a miniature parking lot by the tennis courts she had passed. Who is rich enough to have a parking lot just for their tennis court? The driveway turned into a loop as she approached the house, reminding her of the end of an old-fashioned skeleton key. She stopped her car and listened for a moment. There was nobody around. Nobody should be coming for at least two hours. She had plenty of time.

Like a race-car driver in a film, she sped ahead, spewing gravel out behind her. Her tires must have never have felt so alive, she thought. She pulled up as close as she could to the front door without driving up the stairs of the giant porch. She hit the brakes as if she brake pads were free and she had a pit crew on staff. John's bones hit the inside of the duffel bag and the duffel bag hit the front wall of Laurie's car's trunk. "Sorry John," Laurie called out to the trunk, "I don't know why Honda didn't put a seat belt back there for you."

100 Classic Way was delightfully hidden by beautiful groves. These were the kinds of tree groupings that were meticulously manicured but meant to look natural and effortless, like the liquid and powder makeup dance that many people, particularly women, get up too early in the morning to complete. She pulled up to the house. Six large columns supported the first gable. "We're at the fucking White House, John."

Laurie got out of the car and took a deep breath. Home sweet home. It wasn't her home, but it was pretty sweet and it might as well be hers for the next two hours. Laurie looked out over the professional landscaping and admired the thoughtful clusters of flowers, the rows of cypress trees that encased gardens, and the water features. She wondered if there was a coy pond. She wondered if the home's owner ever fed the fish or if a professional fish technician came to feed them. While she wanted to go looking around the grounds in search of coy, she had to stay focused and handle her business.

First, Laurie unlocked the front door and made her way through the house to the back where the fire pit was waiting. She unlocked all three sets of sliding glass doors and went out onto the enormous deck. She noticed that a few of the deck boards had been recently replaced, but they hadn't been refinished yet. She hoped nobody would show up to refinish them in the next five minutes. "It wouldn't have been smart to unload John's body before determining the best route" she reassured herself while she got the lay of the land. She admired the house's decorative columns and striking mouldings. She walked to the massive fire pit Chris had mentioned. At the bottom left corner, she noticed, there was a small cubby. She slid open the door to the cubby and removed the instruction manual. There was a section for grilling and smoking meats, a section for heating an outdoor space, and a section for decorative flames. Where was the crematorium section? Well. They must have left that one out.

Laurie slid open a large panel at the bottom of the fire pit and looked at the various tanks and compartments. This fire pit made her feel miniature, like she was a toy figurine in an American-Japanese hibachi restaurant and she was preparing for the dinner shift, checking and inspecting the fuel and cleanliness of the grills. She imagined a nineteen-foot tall hibachi chef clanging his spatulas along the top of the smooth and shiny surface of the flat steel plate on top of grill. This fire pit cooking monstrosity combo was almost the size of her living room. Looking up toward the top surface from underneath, she could see that there were different panels that could be rolled out for the different functions of this megalodon of grills. Laurie grabbed the handle attached to the plate that looked most appropriate for the grill's hottest function: decorative ambiance. There was a short list of instructions printed next to each panel. Laurie read the list, located the starter and necessary knobs and then promptly ignored the first step of the setup for decorative ambiance. Instead of clearing the wood chamber of all ashes and debris, she went straight back to her car to retrieve John and his duffel bag. (She figured once your remains are within a duffel bag, it belongs to you, even if it was never one of your possessions.)

John's body and his bag made a satisfying thud when Laurie hoisted him up to the surface of the fire pit and then rolled him toward the center until he dropped down into the wood chamber. Laurie repositioned him from underneath, as if she was putting away cans in an overstuffed pantry. She verified the instructions, positioned all sixteen of the fuel knobs (one for each zone) to begin the flow of the butane, and pressed the starter. Sixteen delightful whooshes happened as the sixteen flame zones ignited and Laurie's face lifted into a smile.

Shit. Laurie's smile fell when she inhaled a gust of smoke. The air smelled so bad. How would she ever hide a burning smell so wretched? Should she leave and come back? Should she leave and not come back? Should she pick up a box of hair dye on her way to running away forever? Surely somebody would catch a whiff of the odorous burning bones, shorts, shoes, and duffel. Shit. Fuck. Shit.

Laurie paced around the yard, oscillating between the idea of running back to her car to drive away and sticking around to supervise the fire pit until the smell went away. Sure enough, after about ten minutes, the black smoke lightened and the chemical odor dissipated. Laurie left the fire pit to do its thing while she started setting up the bar and the few snack items that Chris had purchased. Located on the lowest level of the house, the bar had its own ice machine and there were racks of glassware built into the left side of ceiling over it. Laurie cleared the top of the bar. The workers who had replaced the deck boards had left a cordless drill and a box of deck screws on the bar, so Laurie placed them underneath, next to an empty dish bin and a trash can. Laurie hardly had to do anything other than display the bottles of vodka, gin, rum, and whiskey. Chris had also bought twelve six-packs of Flying Dog beer, in an assorted variety. Laurie put them in the glass-doored fridge next to the bar, trying to arrange the bottles in attractive lines along with sodas and juice for mixing. She opened the basement's sliding glass doors and walked out under the deck. With a deep inhalation, Laurie was unable to smell anything incriminating now. She smiled at the fire pit, which was no longer emitting smoke but displayed a clean troupe of dancing flames and offering a hum of mellifluence. Now that she was feeling more relaxed, she remembered the fire pit's instruction manual having mentioned a feature where the flames synchronize with your music selection. Laurie jogged back to the pit with excitement, streamed the best club-like party mix she could find, and set the fire to move with the beat of the music. The playlist began with Joe Budden's *Fire*. She figured she could change the music later if Chris arrived and wanted a softer vibe.

Every party set-up task that Laurie had thought of was done. She went back to her car to get her bag with some cuter clothes, makeup, and earrings, re-parked so that her old sedan didn't look like a blemish on the mansion's face, and took a quick shower in the guest house by the pool before changing and primping to Usher's *Caught Up*, which was now blaring. She wondering if the flames liked dancing to this or if they preferred something slower.

Chris arrived at the house around 8:20, followed by small groups of people who filtered in every few minutes or so. An Audi full of four attractive people Laurie had never seen before screeched into the driveway around 9:40 and Laurie wondered how Chris knew them. She slowly learned their names without having been introduced because they were just the type of people who collected attention, like solar panels grabbing and storing rays of light. The four of them, like sleek animals who only existed at parties and in dance clubs, made their way to the bar for drinks. As *Bangarang* by Skrillex and Sirah began to play, three of them turned to their fourth friend. The tall guy of the pack who was wearing a black leather jacket said, "Get it, Mari. It's your song. You better do your thing." Mari's three friends took a step back and waited. Mari calmly finished a drink, set it down on the bar, and when the beat of the song dropped, she had landed from a powerful jump into a perfect squat on the bar. Laurie suddenly realized that's what people who do box jumps in the gym are training for. Mari popped up and twerked atop the bar, the triangular bottom tip of her silver sequined bandana-shaped shirt sliding across her abdominal muscles. The whole room, including Laurie, cheered as she danced. Laurie noticed that Mari wasn't looking at the people staring up at her; she had her eyes closed.

Before she knew it, Laurie was enjoying circulating, dancing, drinking, and taking breaks for small talk to catch up with her coworkers. When the playful tune of Robin Thicke's *Blurred Lines* started, Laurie wandered outside toward the fire pit. She found Chris, Shay, and a couple other people relaxing and watching the flames.

"I didn't peg you for a pothead," said Chris. "Can I get in on that? I haven't been high in a decade."

Shay handed him the pipe and cautioned him, "Go slowly. This isn't your regular dirt-weed from high school." Chris exhaled and then drew in a large breath from the pipe. He felt it almost immediately. His heart began to race and he felt lightheaded, so he quickly say down beside Shay.

"Woah. You're right. That's not how I remember weed at all."

Shay replied, "This is my favorite get-up-and-go weed. When I need to wade through a creek of shit I don't want to do, this is what keeps me awake and motivated to get through the work."

"Have you ever shown a house high?" Chris asked.

"Fuck yeah. More often than not, in fact." Said Shay. "The doctor says I need it to ease my anxiety and clear my mind." She paused. "Also, I'm calling myself 'The Doctor' now." Shay laughed and slumped down next to a very high Chris on one of the many padded benches in the fire pit arena.

Laurie took a hit from Shay's pipe and didn't feel anything immediately.

The flames did a two-step as the music changed again. When Laurie looked at Shay, she noticed that Shay's face was streaked with tears.

"Shay, what's wrong?" Laurie asked. Shay didn't respond. She sunk deeper into the pillowy seat. Laurie gently put her arm around Shay. Laurie was never sure what to do in these sorts of situations. Laurie sat uncomfortably while Shay cried on her shoulder.

Chris, who had been absorbed in his smartphone during the eruption of tears, looked up and into the fire. "Wanna go back up to the house for more drinks?" he asked. Shay stood up quickly and discreetly wiped her tears away as best as she could without disturbing the sharp lines of her eyeliner.

"Yeah, bitches. We need more drinks," she said, already leading the way back up to the house.

The three realtor friends made their way up the grassy hill back to the home's basement bar for more alcohol. When they entered, a horde of inebriated guests began to cheer. Laurie was confused, but then remembered that they must be cheering for Chris, who had let them into a multi-millionaire's home and bought enough spirits for all of them to achieve maximum intoxication. A sweaty guy with a vertically striped shirt hooked Chris' neck in his elbow, trying to display him like a trophy but more made him sway back and forth like he was riding a mechanical bull.

The sweaty man raised his bottle of beer with his non-Chris enveloping arm and proclaimed, "A toast to Chris, who is now free! Many men can love a woman, but fewer can escape the trap she's laid for them."

Chris smiled and said, "Thanks, Kevin. And thank you all so much for coming. This really means a lot to me." The crowd waiting for a second to make sure that Chris had reached the conclusion of his short speech before cheering again.

Laurie made herself a gin and tonic while Chris moved through the room and his guests showered him with well-wishes and the occasional comment about "that dumb bitch Bria."

Laurie headed out again with her gin and tonic and looked down over the cobblestone court adjacent to the fire pit arena. She saw a woman from the back wearing a white pants, a hot pink halter top, and a cropped black jacket with matching black stilettos. She must have been very committed to only walking on the balls of her feet in order not to pierce the lawn with every step she made. Any less effort than that and she would have sunk into the ground and caked mud all over her shoes, leaving small holes behind her everywhere she went. Who wears stilettos to an outdoor party? The carefree woman placed her right hand on the shoulder of the tall, muscular man next to her and she extended her fingers, kneading into him. She ran her hand down his chest like she was sensually petting an exotic animal in a music video from the mid 80s. Her arm wrapped around him and she spun herself into him, jumping high and bringing her knees up. His only acceptable response was to catch her, which he did, and she laughed in his face with delight. He smiled and yelled, "Where's the bar?" and then looked into her eyes. The woman jumped out of his basketed arms and grabbed his hand, leading him up toward the house.

"It's this way, baby." She said, walking up the hill with the very attractive man walking his arm's length behind her, like a show poodle on a leash. Oh shit. Laurie hadn't recognized this very familiar woman at first, so she was visibly astonished when she realized that the woman was Peg.

Fucking Peg. Was that her boyfriend? Peg had never talked about a significant other before. Laurie had always assumed that Peg went home to bake weird and barely edible muffins out of things like cloves and rhubarb while trying out new cutesie names for her three disobedient cats who would surely eat her corpse when she died one night sooner or later. Peg and her pet man passed Laurie on the way inside the house. As Peg opened one of the three brilliant sliding glass doors to the home's lower level, she made eye contact with Laurie and smiled. "Toodaloo!"

Laurie couldn't help but whip around and try to see where Peg was going. Peg opened a few doors to closets and a bathroom until she found a bedroom. She grabbed her companion by a fistful of the front of his shirt and tossed him in. Laurie saw the door close behind them and she heard the lock on the door knob turn into place with a low, muffled click. Peg was hooking up. Fucking Peg.

Laurie took informal laps back and forth between the main indoor and outdoor party areas. When something interesting would happen, she would stick around. Upstairs on the deck she passed through people as if she was looking for a friend from whom she had been separated due to partying too hard.

"It's shot o'clock!" yelled Teresa, her hand cupping the side of her mouth, megaphone style. She was carrying a shiny metal tray with eight or nine shot glasses. Naturally, people turned and started to gravitate toward the shots until it seemed like there wouldn't be enough tiny glasses for everyone. Teresa lifted her glass up, raising a toast, "I may not be everyone's cup of tea, but I'm *somebody's* shot of tequila!" She threw her ounce and a half down her throat and then laughed, clearly signaling to the crowd that they should be laughing as well, which they did. Laurie downed her shot of tequila and laughed along as well, out of politeness. Laurie wondered if most people laughed out of politeness, or if most people genuinely thought that all jokes with somebody already laughing along were actually funny. Laurie felt the same way that she usually felt in movie theaters, which was an awkward sense of being unable to enjoy the situation on her own terms. When watching a comedic movie in a movie theater, she always felt like she was being an asshole if she sat silently while the crowd laughed at something she didn't find funny. Conversely, she also felt like an asshole if she laughed audibly at something that she found very funny but nobody else happened to see the humor in. This was one of the reasons that Laurie neither felt completely comfortable at parties nor in movie theaters.

The cacophony of laughter was still ringing in Laurie's ears when she saw him. Shit. Fuck. Shitfuck. She saw a man in a blue button down shirt and black slacks who happened to be Mark. She froze. She broke her stare at him and tried to look anywhere else. She realized that avoiding looking at all in his direction was also very weird and she tried to remember how much time a normal person would spend looking at any other person about whom she did not care at all. Laurie felt embarrassed. She placed her shot glass back on Teresa's silveresque tray and her embarrassment began to turn into something else: rage. Her fingers felt hot and the heat expanded, traveling up her arms, spreading from her armpits down to her trunk and legs, reaching her toes. Like a wildfire, she couldn't contain it.

Laurie turned away to hide her confusion and anger. A tear welled up in her left eye and she wiped it away with her forearm, trying to hide her emotional leakage and attempting to keep her eyeliner in tact. She walked to the downstairs bar and poured herself a vodka on the rocks. While she sipped, the coldness of the chilled liquor rolling down her esophagus helped her distress congeal into a solid confidence. She was forming a plan, but her knowing how careful she had to be kept her from thinking in words, as if the people around her might be able to hear her thoughts if she thought them too plainly and clearly. Laurie thought in images, making her plans, each one an isolated frame of the upcoming slasher film that would become her busy night.

Laurie kept sipping her drink, keeping her ears alert and staying out of Mark's view. She started to calm herself more. Without having to turn her head, she knew that Mark and his crew had wandered out onto the deck and meandered down the stairs to the basement bar area. Laurie floated into a narrow hallway around the side of the bar. She listened from around the corner.

"So what are you doing after this?" asked Zeke, apparently a friend of Mark's.

"Hopefully, her." Mark said, indicating a woman with curly brown shoulder-length hair and three shiny buttons in a vertical line at the center of breast pleats in her black a-line tank top with thick shoulder straps. Her thighs were poured into light blue denim and her muffin top and thick lips looked soft and approachable. Laurie loved her style. She didn't know the woman's name, but in her mind she called her Margot.

"You oughta be able to bag that. I'm a little surprised you're not going for something a little more top shelf." Said Zeke with genuine drunk bro honesty.

"Naw, I like 'em thick and ready. I'm tired, man. I don't want to work that hard and girls like that will do pretty much anything and you can toss 'em around a little without breaking them."

Zeke pointed out a thinner woman with a similar outfit by tilting his head toward her and told Mark, "Now that's a fox right there. That's what I want."

Mark laughed and told him, "But see Zeke you're prolly not gonna get her. You're gonna go home alone. My fat fox is much easier to trap because she's not about to be running away."

Laurie winced in disgust until she heard an abrupt cackle, a thud, and the swing of a door opening. Peg paraded out of the downstairs bedroom with her man-candy trotting behind her. She heard another door swing open. Laurie peeked around the corner to see that Margot had just entered the tiny bathroom down the hall. Laurie thought quickly. Was there a window in there? Yes! There was! Was the window big enough for Margot to climb through? Probably. Well, maybe. If not, Margot would at least be able to open it and yell for assistance. Laurie swooped from the hallway to behind the bar and retrieved the cordless drill and a handful of deck screws that she had remembered seeing while she was tidying up. She darted back down the hallway and screwed three screws through the bathroom's door jamb and into the door. She put the screw gun back behind the bar, smoothed her shirt, and headed toward Mark.

Chapter Seven

End the Conversation First

"Hey. I know you," Mark said playfully. Laurie took a large breath in but tried to keep her pulse from rising. She told herself she was relaxed.

"Oh? And what do you remember about me?" Laurie asked, swirling her drink and biting the side of her bottom lip while locking in Mark's eyes. Laurie emulated the gestures that a lead character in a romantic comedy would model. She was poised, yet flowy. She tossed her head around, almost like a helium-filled balloon trying to escape its dainty string. This was a meetcute, except that they weren't meeting for the first time and it didn't feel cute for either of them.

"I remember your beautiful face and I remember you could do magic with your tongue." Mark said, taking a chance.

"Gross." Laurie thought to herself. She kept the disgust below her throat and didn't let it fly up to her face for expression to share with the party. Instead, she released a tiny laugh and then took a step toward him as she asked him playfully, "Oh yeah?"

"And what do you remember about me?" He asked her, taking a huge swig from his cup. What time was it? Laurie glanced to the side of the room to see a large clock's digital display of 10:45. Mark looked tired. She wouldn't have to put herself on a hook and then slowly lure him in. If this were going to work, her best bet would be to jump in the water and grab him right now.

Like a ballet dancer mid-tendu, she dragged her back foot forward and then lifted her toe and stepped next to his feet and wrapped her free arm up over his shoulder, warmly half-hugging him to whisper in his ear, "I remember... that you you fucked me so hard and so good." Laurie could gauge from his exhalation that he was into it and she continued, "And I want you to give me your hard cock again tonight." She carefully drew back and smiled with innocence as if she had just told him, "I like your shirt" or "You have pretty eyes."

Mark grabbed her hand and twirled her so that he was against the back of her body. He lowered his head and slobbered a little on her ear while he whispered, "Let's get the fuck out of here, baby." He then bent his knees slightly so he could tilt his hips up. His hardening dick raised slightly to her warmth, trying to burrow under her posterior. She pulled his arms over hers and threaded her fingers through his, hugging herself from the back with his arms. She turned toward him again, bringing his hands to her upper back. She put two fingers in his left front pocket and pulled his waist toward her. She planted her other hand on his right cheek and cradled his face while she planted a deeply sensual kiss on his whole mouth, playing with his bottom lip as she pulled away. He made an involuntary soft grunt. She glided her hand down his chest and then took his hand and led him up the stairs, dodging party guests and they walked toward the front door where her car was parked. They skipped all sensical logistics-based questions concerning who should drive and what their destination was and who had consumed fewer drinks and they got into Laurie's car as if they had robbed the house they were just in. Before Laurie put her seat belt on, she leaned over and gave Mark another kiss, this time on his neck. She went in softly, as if her lips were blotting a mild wound and then she traced his neck muscles and his lower jaw with her tongue. His head rolled back against the headrest and he moaned, "Oh fuck. Baby, let's go home."

"Would you like a beer?" Laurie asked? Mark nodded and Laurie grabbed a beer from her refrigerator. She opened her utensil drawer to retrieve the bottle opener and her fingers lingered over her spoons, forks, and knives. How was she going to do this? Her eyes darted up to her knife block on the counter by the stove. Which one?

Mark finished three quarters of his beer almost immediately. He set the almost-empty bottle on the counter. "Where's your bathroom?" he asked her.

"It's this door right here," Laurie said, pointing to one of two doors in her kitchen. "That door's the half-bath and that door's the pantry," she explained. When Mark beelined for the bathroom, Laurie smiled. How did that happen so easily. She was thinking she would have to stall Mark in the kitchen with possibly several beers until he had to take a piss, but he completed this part of her plan himself. Wow. Laurie blinked.

The two knives from the butcher block felt lighter in her fists than she had remembered them feeling while she was chopping, mincing, or slicing in her kitchen, and the steel handles were pleasantly cold in her sweaty palms. After squeezing them with the blades facing up, she reversed the handles so the blades were facing down, just to feel the coolness on her hands as she took a deep breath. Laurie had quickly chosen the santoku knife and the long, serrated bread knife without much reasoning. On her way to the couch, she thought about how she might have chosen the chef's knife and a paring knife, or maybe one of the steak knives or one of the three knives for which she didn't know the names. Laurie stepped lightly and tried not to make a sound. The cloth of her sofa rubbed against her knuckles as she stashed both knives in the crevice where the seat cushions met the back cushions. Laurie hoped none of her cushions would be sliced in this endeavor. She tip-toed back to the kitchen and paced while wondering if she could buy new covers for couch cushions online. Mark finished peeing. Laurie heard him run the water in the sink for five seconds, which wasn't nearly enough time to fully wash his hands. She wondered if he had even passed his hands under the stream of water. Disgusting. On the other hand, if in his mind Laurie was about to touch his penis, should the touching of his own penis really warrant a full hand-washing? Maybe Mark had a point. A debate between Laurie and Mark over handwashing before sex took place in Laurie's mind. How dirty was the shaft of a penis anyway? How frequently did men get accidental drops of urine on their hands? The door opened. Laurie met him in the doorway of her powder room and kissed him deeply. She reached her right hand up to his face and then slid it down onto his upper chest, where she had softly placed her other hand. She let her fingers run down him until her index fingers met his front belt loops. She marched backward, tugging him along with her to the couch. They did a 180 turn, like two middle schoolers at a dance in their cafeteria so that Mark's back was facing the couch and Laurie could sexily push him down and then climb on top of him. Before Mark sat, he paused.

Shit. Did he know? Did he noticed the knives missing from the knife block? Laurie took a step back. Mark casually removed his phone, keys, and wallet from his pants' pockets, tossed them beside the sofa and then held his hands out, a cue for Laurie to resume. Whew. They collapsed on the couch and kissed. Mark began to tug at Laurie's shirt, a wordless request for removal, when they heard a buzz. It was Mark's phone vibrating.

Mark bent over the side of the couch to pick up his phone and Laurie grasped the serrated bread knife from the couch. She stood up on the couch, held the knife high over her head, and then brought it down as hard as she could into his back with all of the force she could muster. Did she get his heart? Where was his heart? Which side was the heart on again? His left or the left of somebody facing him? Oh no. What if the job wasn't done? Maybe she should have thought this through more. Mark let out a grunty scream and Laurie panicked. Mark turned over and Laurie reacted instinctively, shoving the knife as far as she could through his right eyeball and into his brain. Laurie had never wanted to know about the consistency of vitreous fluid, but she would never be able to un-learn how Mark's eye jelly glopped down his face. "Ew. Don't eat that, Mark," she whispered as some of it ran into his mouth. Fuck. She would probably have to buy new couch-cushion covers.

On the way in to Lowe's the next morning at 6:14, Laurie chucked Mark's powered-off phone, his keys, and his wallet into the large trashcan outside. She had washed them carefully in the sink and put them in a plastic grocery bag, which she had also washed. She was careful to only handle the clean bag of Mark's items with a second plastic bag, which Laurie shoved back into her purse.

"What's so special about ceiling paint?" Laurie wondered, wandering through aisles of Lowe's. "Wasn't it just white paint? And for that matter, what was so special about primer? Wasn't that also essentially white paint?" She parked her cart on the edge of the aisle so she couldn't possibly obstruct anybody who might wander down the aisle browsing rollers or putty knives before pressing the home button, unlocking her phone. Her search of paints and their specificities pulled her into a world of viscosity and the gradient of sheens available.

"Can I help you find something?" Tibor asked. He had lumbered down the aisle taskless toward Laurie and stopped, just as Laurie had hoped he wouldn't.

"Thank you so much, but I think I'm all set," she said, meeting his dark eyes. Tibor's eyelashes were wet and bold, adding a deer-like sense of youth to his retail-stressed body, belly unsuccessfully shuttered by his red and blue vest and poking over the top of his workpants, like a large pumpkin atop a tiny bucket.

"What are you painting?" Tibor asked.

"Oh, um, just trying to freshen up the house."

"Okay. Well if you need help finding anything, I'll be close by."

"Thank you. I appreciate it." Tibor continued down the aisle with uneven steps, as if his right leg were two inches shorter than the left one. A man whirled around the corner and halted, joining them in the paint aisle. The man whistled what sounded like the refrain of Fergie's *London Bridge* as he tossed a contractor pack of blue painters' tape into his cart. Tibor disappeared around the corner without acknowledging him. Laurie quickly grabbed a gallon of white primer, a gallon of white ceiling paint, and headed back to the service counter, hoping the attendant had finished mixing her requested color.

As well as her specific can of paint, the attendant handed her the small chip of the wall that she had provided as the color sample. "Thank you so much," she said, remembering that she also needed some spackling and sandpaper in order to fix the little hole she had chiseled out with a butter knife that morning. She grabbed the last items, checked out, and hurried to her car. The sooner she could get to work, the better.

Laurie didn't have a tarp, so she cut up some plastic shopping bags and placed them on the floor to protect the carpet from paint. She stirred the primer and tested it out on one of the stains. The blood was still very visible through the coat of primer as it dried, so she worked at the splattered dots, grinding them down with some of the sandpaper. Much better. She finished painting quickly, leaving two hours to dry between coats of primer and paint.

"Not bad," she said aloud six hours later, admiring the now clean wall. She washed and put away her tools, storing them along with the remainder of the paint. She retrieved a glass of cold water from her kitchen then sat on the floor with her legs crossed in a minute of rest. Now it was time for the hard part. Mark was draped over the toilet, his neck bleeding into the bowl. Laurie had flushed the toilet quite a few times, but it just seemed to fill up again and again. At least he'd be a little lighter to lift once the sun had set and she could transfer his body to the car.

Laurie knew where Mark could go. The landscaping at 3345 Orvis Way was so fresh, so manicured, that nobody would notice that the dark and earthy mulch blanketing the new rose garden was just a couple inches higher than it was the day before. Mark could rest under the roses. Romantic.

Laurie continued drinking cold water as the satisfying sweat of a hard day's work dripped down her back. She picked up her phone and called Chris, who answered on the first ring. "Hey Chris?" Laurie said, "The deal's off. I'm sorry. I'll still bring you bagels tomorrow. I'll call the settlement company right after we hang up. Again, I'm sorry." Chris was silent for a moment. Then he scoffed. Laurie braced herself for a lecture about how much work he had put into getting ready for this sale and he'd have nothing to show for it, but instead he told her, "Laurie, I'm so happy you're not going through with this. It's not your job to fix The Shit Hole. You'll find a nice house to live in and you won't be paying for it after after the mortgage is over." Laurie smiled and she felt a weight lift from her shoulders.

Showings of the house on Orvis Way ended at nine o'clock, but Laurie knew that nobody would be home. The Muellers had both retired and had already stationed themselves in Florida for their remaining years, heavily scheduled with margaritas, movies, and sitting by the pool. Their home didn't seem like theirs anymore. Inside wasn't their blender, their sofa, their barstools, or their bedding. The home was staged professionally and no longer contained any belongings of theirs, but was instead adorned with specifically chosen home furnishings that were clean and sleek, all deliberately placed in such a way to make prospective home buyers think that if they could just move into a home like this, then their lives would be so organized, free of clutter, and unbound by any of their current problems.

Laurie parked in the driveway. She had written the code for the lockbox in her showings notebook. She carefully entered the code from the home tour she had given a few days ago, retrieved the key, unlocked the door, and carefully entered the house.

"Right this way through the kitchen to the dining area. The most modern of floor plans, this one incorporates a half-wall. The completely open home concept that has dominated home architecture for the last twenty years is on its way out."

"Aw, shit," Laurie thought. "Fucking Peg." Peg was in fact floating through the house, though she was supposed to have been gone fifteen minutes ago. A bored couple shuffled behind her. They had already gotten as much out of the home tour as they had wanted and were beginning to resent Peg's endless anecdotes for each room. Brenda and Jared, or whatever their names were, surely would have had a much more comfortable experience if they hadn't had to hear Peg dramatically drone on about the home owner's grandmother who stared out of her bedroom window for five hours each morning and found solace in the view of Sugarloaf Mountain off in the distance, her only remedy for grief she had been carrying since her husband's passing.

Trying to silently exit and come back after Peg and her

clients were gone would be too risky. Laurie would have to own her entrance. "Hi! It's Laurie! I'm here a little early to set up for my 9:15- Just didn't want to scare you!"

"Oh! My! What time is it?" Peg bumbled.

"I didn't see any tours after 8:30 on the schedule," Laurie said in her best apologetic, non-intrusive tone.

"Well I didn't see you on the schedule at all, so I thought we could take our time. Isn't that right, folks?" Peg said, looking to Brenda and Jared for support.

"Actually," Brenda started, "We've really got to get going. Our sitter is probably wondering where we are. This home is lovely though. We'll check in with you tomorrow."

"Ah, well, toodaloo!" Peg chirped as she opened the door to let the young couple out.

"I'll be sure to lock everything up and close out for the night," Laurie assured Peg.

"Oh! Okay! Well then! And what type of clients do you have coming to see this lovely gem?"

"Gay. Dudes. Small dog. Matching sweaters."

"Enjoy!" Peg chanted while exiting the house with an unnaturally long stride, pointing her toes with each step and letting the rest of her body follow, her asymmetrical linen tunic flowing as she did.

Laurie watched Peg disappear into the neighborhood streets.

Laurie was about to carefully replace the soil and newly installed bushes over Mark's body. She was already thinking about returning her shovel back to the home's unlocked shed, when she saw something move out of the corner of her eye. Squirrel? No. It was a fox. The fox trotted like a waterfall, powerful and fluid, adaptive and light, but forceful. She thought that she had better go inside, but something kept her there. The fox tilted up its nose and its eyes met hers. It told her not to leave, just yet.

"Rabies" the logical part of Laurie's brain told her. "About twenty percent of foxes submitted for testing had rabies." She had better get inside, she thought, but instead she followed a strange and irrational feeling. The fox wanted her to stay.

Rabies kills people. But wait, wasn't there a vaccine? Who gets a rabies vaccine? Laurie was pretty sure that wasn't something she was protected from. The overwhelming majority of rabies deaths were in Africa and Asia in parts of the world that weren't at all like hers. She stayed, without explanation to herself. The fox tatted over to her. It lifted up its nose daintily, a request for something she could help it with. "What is it?" She asked the creature.

The fox lifted a paw and brushed her knee ever so gently.

They locked eyes, and then the fox pointed to the hole with its nose.

"You want to say goodbye?"

The fox turned back to Laurie, eyes watering. "What do you want, little fox?" she asked. The fox pointed at Laurie's spade-tipped shovel with her paw.

Somehow, Laurie knew what to do. She picked up the shovel and hovered the tip over Mark's chest. Mark looked so peaceful, all alone in the dirt with his one remaining eye and the blood on his gaping throat having coagulated enough to no longer drip. She looked at the fox to verify. The dainty fox nodded and Laurie brought the shovel's sharp point down into Mark's chest, slashing through him and breaking his sternum.

"Well, go on, Roberta," Laurie told the fox, unsure if the

creature would accept the name Laurie gave her or not. Roberta crouched forward and lowered her pointy nose into Mark's burial hole. She thrust her face into the crater in Mark's chest. His body had cooled down completely since late last night; he felt tepid and clumpy, like a pasta salad left outside at a spring picnic. The fox assured Laurie that she was doing the right thing by letting out a tiny yip, muffled by Mark's ribs. She gripped Mark's heart in her teeth and whimpered an appreciative confirmation, which Laurie accepted. The fox grasped Mark's heart and pulled. With jaws like pruning loppers, Roberta nipped the vena cava, satisfyingly severing it. Delectable. Roberta slowly climbed out of the hole and tore into the organ with audible rips. She swallowed it in seven bites and trotted off.

* * *

Made in the USA
Coppell, TX
23 November 2024